CHESS STORIES' THROUGH THE AGES

By

DONALD BOONE

Other books by this author

The Art of Playing Chess

Those Who Play Chess

The Scholastic Chess Coach

The Chess Game

The Chess Set

Chess Records

INTRODUCTION

In this revised edition of this book you will read stories from the past. Historical knowledge is the basis for these tales and it may come from past decades, to centuries in times past. Stories that should be of some interest to every chess player.

The men and women who play chess are indeed Kings and Queens of the game. They are often treated as chess royalty as they progress higher into the world of the chess master ratings as well. Mentally they seem above and beyond the thinking of those of us who cannot see far enough into a chess match to know of the outcome before we reach the end game.

Chess stories abound, but rarely found in one source for one's reading pleasure. Anyone who plays the game of chess will find this book of interest. Perhaps even to the extent that they will discover how some things in the game came into being. Chess is a game that brings extreme interest as you learn more of its in intricacies, and yes, to some, captivating, or perhaps, even addictive.

IN THIS BOOK

THE FAMILY SQUABBLE

The afternoon had gone as rapidly as the morning, at least for Theodore. With the heavy rain coming down for hours on end, he'd been forced to stay indoors. This was on orders from his mother and his grandmother. The two of them were in the sewing room, and in the process of making him a new quilt for his bed. Because he hadn't found anything of entertaining interest in that room, he began to roam about.

He'd gone to the kitchen next, but, Martha, the cook, had shooed him out of there as she was making preparations for the coming dinner hour. From there he'd gone to the attic, a place he'd spent countless hours exploring over the past few weeks.

He knew spring was on its way, but it still seemed too far away. In the spring he could explore the whole of his grandfather's large estate. His father was away on the mainland tending to some of his grandfather's shipping business, and this was the reason he and his mother had elected to spend the winter months with his grandparents.

Tiring of the attic adventure, he decided to look for his grandfather. He was sure he could be found in the den. He knocked at the large dark wooden door leading into the room where his grandfather spent most of his daylight hours.

From inside he heard, "Come."

The room was not dark, but it was not well lit either. The walls were lined with bookcase after bookcase. A rolling ladder was attached to a rail on the top of the tall book cases and could easily be moved from one location to another. He'd tried riding on it one afternoon, when he and his mother had come in to ask his grandfather something, but his grandfather had scolded him for doing so.

As he entered the room, he was aware of the large lamp and it was the only source of light on his grandfather's dark, heavy, teak wood desk.

"Ah. . . .Teddy, my lad. What are you up to this afternoon?"

"There's nothing to do around here today, Grandpa pa."

"I see. So you're bored, is that it?"

"Yes sir."

"Well, I've almost finished what few items I needed to take care of, so why don't you give me a few minutes then perhaps we can find something to do together?"

"Okay, Grandpa pa."

While he waited for his grandfather, he began to look around the room. This was not his first time here, but the first time he felt comfortable wandering around in a room so full of interesting things.

Soon he spied a very ornate box on a shelf just slightly above eye level. The box was of highly polished red lacquer. The corners were covered with molded brass fittings, and he could just see brass hinges peeking out of the seam on the back of the box.

He could see another brass plate of some kind on the front, but it was obscured by a short, thick book with the name of 'Philidor,' gracing its red leather cover in gold print. Next to that one was another book bound in black leather. The name on that one was, 'Steintz.'

Quietly he rolled the ladder down closer so he could see the box more clearly, and in so doing he found the top of the box to be inlaid with Mother of Pearl. The design seemed rather familiar to him. He'd seen something like it before, he thought it might be on a special chest his grandmother favored. She kept it in her bedroom, it having been brought home from China.

On each side of the box on the shelf before him were books. Some were, what he knew to be Biographies of famous people, people he was unfamiliar with. Others were of history, titles with the words' Persia, India, China and Japan on them.

This did not surprise him as he knew his grandfather's shipping company spent many months in those lands buying and selling wares.

He knew he should not touch the box, but his curiosity was overwhelming. Carefully, after looking over his shoulder to see if he was being watched, he pushed the closest thick book ever so slightly.

Just enough so that he could see what was on the front of the box. Revealed to his eyes was a small hole in the brass plate, a hole that would accept a key. It was a lock.

He stepped down from the step of the ladder and walked to the side of his grandfather's desk, where he stood close by his chair, waiting patiently. His grandfather lifted his eyes to meet those of his cherished grandson.

"Yes, Teddy."

"Grandpa pa. What's in that red box on the shelf over there?" He turned and pointed with fingers that looked as though they belonged on a musician.

His grandfather turned to face him. The base of the oak swivel chair squeaked slightly as he did so. He did not speak to Teddy for a few moments, as if lost in thought. Then he answered with one word, and one word only. "Danger."

The moment seemed to last far longer than it had, neither of them speaking further about the box, when a knock came at the door. It opened slightly as his mother poked her head into the room.

"Dinner is ready. Come on you two,"

That night the box haunted his memory, he had to know what was inside. He would ask his grandfather about it again in the morning.

Late, after he'd breakfasted, he approached the den, the door was ajar, as if his grandfather was expecting someone. He knocked just the same, pushed the door open slowly, and heard his name being said.

"Teddy. I've been expecting you."

His grandfather reached for a bell that he knew would signal the kitchen. In moments Martha came into the room. "You sent for me, Sir?"

"Martha, if you would kindly bring us a hot cider, and perhaps a cookie or two."

After Martha had left them, his grandfather said. "You've still a question?"

Teddy summoned his courage, then blurted out. "Is the box so dangerous that you cannot show me what's inside?"

Again a few moments of silence while his grandfather fidgeted in his chair. His hand raised up to smooth the silver hair back on his head, then came to rest under his chin, as if to support his head while pondering the question of endangering this favorite grandchild.

Finally, he made up his mind, saying. "I'll have to speak to your mother before we go further."

"When, grandpa pa?"

"After dinner this evening. You will have to be patient."

Martha came with the cider and cookies, but even as he consumed them, his mind was still on the red box on the shelf nearby.

In the evening he watched, with great anticipation, as his mother was beckoned by his grandfather to follow him into his study. Teddy, tried to listen, but he could not hear their words clearly. He knew his mother was objecting, but not strenuously. Their voices were not raised, and this, he reasoned, was a good sign. Still, it was a squabble of sorts and unheard of in this home. Apparently his mother had come near the door as he listened and was about to leave the room. He heard her say, "If you're sure it is okay to show him the things in that box, go ahead. They haven't killed you. . . . yet."

Teddy just had enough time to get away from the door, but as his mother exited the room, she saw him nearby and as she smiled at him, he was sure she knew he had been close to the door while she was speaking with his grandfather.

"He's waiting for you. You pay attention to what he tells you."

"Yes, mother."

As he entered the den, his grandfather said, "Close the door behind you. You and I will be dealing with the world of men, past and present."

His grandfather, who had been standing in the center of the room when he entered, said. "Here, help me move this table over in front of the fireplace."

He'd seen the table before. It, too, was ornate. Mother of pearl inlays decorated it along each side. The table being held aloft by legs of Rosewood and golden studs to fasten all of it together. He thought it was only for playing Draughts upon its surface of ebony and ivory squares. He was about to learn that it was for another game as well.

With the table settled in front of the fireplace his grandfather placed a lamp on the mantel so it would light the board's surface. Then he said. Teddy, get the box from the shelf. Then you will find a gold key in the small partition on the left side of my center desk drawer.

As he carried the box ever so carefully, he had to force his hands not to shake, fearing he might drop it and unleash the powers it held inside. He gave the box to his grandfather, then retrieved the key as instructed.

Seated in a chair on one side of the table, his grandfather indicated that he should sit in the chair opposite to him on the other side of the table.

7

When he was settled, his grandfather placed the box on the table top, inserted the key into the lock and turned it until they both heard the small click it made, releasing the lid to be lifted by a daring hand.

His eyes marveled at the pieces of gold and silver as each was removed from the box, and as his grandfather explained the name of each piece, he committed the names of each of them to memory. Over the next few hours, of that first evening, and the many days to follow, he learned what was expected of each of the marvelous pieces that had lain dormant in the box which had been kept on the shelf of his grandfather's bookcase.

Years would go by before he understood the reality of the danger that his grandfather had warned him about. The danger comes from the complete absorption of one's mind and not only while playing the game. He learned the game of chess had completely swallowed some men's minds, and their lives as well. With a few their physical health would suffer, some not even changing clothes for days on end as they tried to fathom the depth of a tricky chess move they had been exposed too in a chess tournament.

It was not the contents of the ornate box that were of danger. It was the capturing of the minds of mankind.

THE PHONE CALL

I've been involved in so many chess events that at times I confuse one for another. However, If I remember correctly, it was the New York Master's Tournament at which I had been a volunteer helper, in my case I was little more than a messenger boy. Still, this allowed me to be present in the area of games being played. As I was meandering around the main room, I saw a player sitting by himself at a chessboard and without an opponent.

Curious, I asked the tournament director about my observations, and he said. "That is Capablanca's table, and, as usual, he is late."

I knew that when a player is late he has an hour to appear at his board and begin to play, so I asked. "So, do you know where he is?"

"No. I do not, but I have started his clock."

So I watched his clock, as did his opponent. It was down to forty minutes when his opponent got up and disappeared for a short time.

I only assumed he had gone to the lavatory, but I found I may have been wrong in that assumption. The clock continued counting off the minutes, forty five minutes passed and still no Capablanca.

With nine minutes left on his clock he hurried into the room and to his table, his hand quickly making his first fifteen moves with speed that resembled . . .Hmmm . . . lightening. By doing so he was still safely within his time limits.

Taking advantage of my acceptance in the room I had moved closer to observe what took place, and I'm not sure, but I think I heard Capablanca say. "Thank you for phoning me. I might have lost this game by default had you not done so."

THE FRENCH UNDERGROUND

During the second world war the German army commandeered a chateau in Pas-de-Calais. The family who lived there at the time were allowed to stay, but as servants to the German officers who took the better rooms of the chateau for themselves.

It was during a late evening that the German General who commandeered the area, happened across the man who had been in the employ of the family as a tutor for the families children, and he was playing chess with one of his charges. The officer watched the game in progress and asked to play a game with him after his current game ended. He acknowledged that he would be honored. He wasn't of course, but to refuse could mean death. This in turn, was to be the first of many nightly games between the two men.

Things began to take place in the area that caused rumors to spread through the village quickly, and became widely known. Wide enough that those in England took notice. Word reached the allied forces from the French underground that there were secret plans in a safe in the German general's quarters in the house in which he was living.

A plan was quickly put in place by the allies. A message was passed along to the tutor. He was given a time and date on which to play chess with the General. He was to understand that he had to keep the general involved in the game for at least an hour.

The tutor, himself also knew the only way into the general's quarters was through a window very high from the ground, and that it could only be entered from the roof of the chateau. On the night the planned game took place, it was very windy with a heavy storm passing through the area.

Usually the tutor could easily beat the German general at the game, but during this game he could not afford too win quickly, he had to drag the game out as long as he could. He blocked his own pieces with his Pawns and lost a Bishop through a seemingly careless move.

This resulted in the General's mind becoming completely absorbed in the game, to the extent that odd noises didn't seem to register with him, or were dismissed as being caused by the high winds. The tutor's King was forced to move, thus preventing him from castling, leaving it vulnerable to attack. It soon became apparent that the General was close to announcing check mate, but it was still too early to let the game come to a close. He had to stall as long as he could.

The tutor discovered a Pawn move that could slow the coming defeat, and moved it one square to intercept the General's attack. This brought the General's mind deeper into the game as it had been wandering as he grew impatient.

One noise caught the General's attention and he got up from his seat at the table, then walked to the door of his quarters, looked inside the room, but saw nothing amiss, and returned to the game.

It only took the General a few more moves, and the loss of his own Queen, but he did win the game.

As it happened, a few days later British bombers flew over the area and destroyed everything in the surroundings. The result was the new German secret facility no longer existed.

NO WINNER, NO LOSER

In the south of France, and in a small museum's vault, is an unusual chess set. The reason this chess set is kept here, is its value. It's valuable in the sense that it is worthless. First let me explain a few things about the chess set itself.

The board squares are of Ebony for the black squares and the white squares are Mother of Pearl. The entire board is held together with a bronze base and supported on bronze feet. Though the board is outstanding, it is the pieces that really capture your mind. The white pieces are of bleached elephant tusk ivory. The darker pieces are of walrus tusks. The pieces representing the Kings are slightly rounded outward in the middle, as if they have had little to do, but dine. If you spread your three central fingers apart, you will see their height. At the top of his, royal majesty, and just below the edge, is a wide crown carved in a style of Scrimshaw. The Queen is similar, but her crown is a bit thinner in height. The scrimshaw on all of the pieces appears as though it was done by a skilled craftsman. Perhaps even a seaman roaming the world for most of his life. The Rooks are fairly straight up the sides, but carry a sword and coat of arms on each. The tops of these pieces bear two cuts across the top and at right angles to one another. These lines appear to have been cut with a fine-toothed saw. The Bishops are tapered cylinders but with what appears to be a Cardinal's hat at the top, but they are not pointed. The Knights, depict a Knight's helmet and the same coat of arms carved in scrimshaw as that of the Rooks. The

Pawns are of smaller tapered shape, but also bear a cross on each, as if leading the King's army on its way into battle. Finally, at the top of each piece appears an imbedded stone. One of an unusual nature. A stone unlike any you've seen before. These are stones that are similar to others that have all been found in odd places. One of those documented locations, was inside a lump of coal while a woman was breaking lumps of coal up for her morning fire. Others have been found in various locations, none of them the same.

The odd thing about this chess set is that no one can lose the game. Well, in a similar sense, no one is able too win a game either. Those who have played chess with this set each confer the same thing after attempting to be successful at winning a game with this chess set. It goes something like this.

"You cannot make a bad move. It's as if the pieces have a mind of their own and guide you to the place they should be played on each move. You can start the game in any manner of your choosing, but even then you cannot make an error."

The opposing player agrees, saying. "You make moves as if being told what, and how to move." To the point that the game ends up a stalemate or a draw as everyone has played a perfect game.

Apparently just touching the pieces gives the players a sense of power. The power is not in the player's hands, but comes from the pieces themselves. As if the imbedded stones contain a memory as to what should take place each time. As if they feel, or see the game taking place before it does take place. Like that of a Master chess player who studies the game beforehand. Now you can understand why the chess set is worthless.

It is only a rumor, but it si said that a Mackeïdes, the son of battle, made the set. Still, many would like to possess it for their own.

NOTE:

My past research leads me to think the stones mentioned in this story may be similar to something known as a Parallelepiped. If this is the case, these stones can measure from small to several centimeters per side. I'm to understand the stones are like memory chips, and that it may be possible for them to store the data of all mankind for the last 10 million years. These Parallelepiped items are iron cubes, or some similar metal as far as is known. They have been found in solid rock, and coal that are millions of years old. They have been found from the 1600s to the 1900s. Measuring one sq. inch = 6.45 sq. centimeter by 1 centimeter = 0.394 inch. Am I saying that is what these stones in this chess set are? No, I am not, but the similarity is surprising.

AN END GAME

When Akiba Rubinstien took an interest in chess, his, only source of information about the game was in a book he'd found written completely in Hebrew. He was able to read the book, but it took him awhile but he memorized the entire book.

He started to climb up the social ladder in the chess world, but it came to an abrupt halt because of the outbreak of the first world war. However, even before that had happened he'd competed in twenty-three major tournaments.

Four years later, and when Capablanca was at the height of his powers, Akiba was beginning to show signs of mental stress and some sickness, which, in the long run, resulted in his complete withdrawal from chess.

During his climb to the high status of becoming an International Grand Master he'd introduced many innovations to the game in the opening moves, also in the end game he had no equal. It had been said of him that "To enter the end game with Rubinstein, was to court disaster."

As with many men of great mental skill, he showed signs of eccentricity. After he'd made a move during a chess match, he would leave the table and would not come back to the chess board until it was his move again.

There were those that thought that apparently he did this so as not to disturb his opponents thinking process. During one game he was so lost in thought that he stopped in the hotels dining room for lunch. Finished, he rose from the table, his mind back on the game. Walking aimlessly through the building deep in thought, he came to a door marked, 'Dining Room.' Where upon he entered, sat down and ordered lunch forgetting he'd just finished eating.

As his mental illness progressed he began to suffer from a persecution mania and became more and more withdrawn. After retiring from chess he spent some time in a Sanatorium. He recovered and went to Brussels to live. At the end of his life, he died in an old people's home.

THE EVAN'S GAMBIT

In the year of 1870, The good Captain Evans was living with his daughter and son in Ostend Holland. He was living on a small pension under strained circumstances, but getting by. As it happened, at the time, the Grand Duke, 'Nicholas' was visiting the area in Bruges during that season. This was about sixteen miles from the captain, and he had been informed that the Captain lived nearby. The Grand Duke was himself, an avid chess player and knew of the Gambit this particular man had come up with. With this in mind, he offered an invitation to the Captain join him in a game of chess. When the invitation arrived at his son's home, his son, and daughter, were overwhelmed. The conversation between the father and son, went something like this.

"Father, the Grand Duke has asked that you come to play chess with him. How wonderful."

The old man was silent for a spell, then said. "Balderdash, I'll not go."

His children were astounded, and his son said. "You'll not go. What are you saying? It's the Grand Duke who has summoned you."

His father still refused, mumbling something about debts unpaid. When the invitation arrived a second time, the old man still refused to attend.

It was the third time, and when the Duke had sent some of his personal Aides-de-camp, with instructions to bring the old man whether he wanted to come or not, that Captain Evans gave in and consented to go along.

The old sailor, and one of the greatest autocrats in history, met to play chess. The old man of the sea was well cared for while in the Dukes dwelling, well fed, and spoiled beyond anything he knew to be normal. They played a hard long game, one that lasted three days and in the end, the old salt won the game. At the end of the game, the Grand Duke said to him.

"I believe you invented the Evans Gambit?"

"Aye, Sir. And, it is not the only thing I have invented for which you have not paid me."

The Duke, somewhat bemused, as he had not expected to pay for a game of chess, replied.

"What is the other?"

"I invented the navigation lights your ships use. Red for Port, Green for Starboard." He was well aware that the Grand Duke was at the time Admiral of the Russian navy.

Nothing more was said at the time and Captain Evans returned to his residence in Ostend. Some months later he received a letter from the Russian Consul asking him to come by the consulate at his leisure.

When he arrived at the consulate, he was given a letter from the Grand Duke Nicholas.

The letter explained how happy the Duke had been to have made his acquaintance, and to have played chess with him.

After having read the letter, he was also given a gold chronometer with the inscription on the obverse that said, "To the great and good man, William Evans," On the reverse side were two engraved ships with their lights represented with precious stones. The gold chain with the watch representing each link in a ship's anchor.

He also received a large cash settlement in payment for Russia's right to use the lights for navigation.

THE MASTER AMATEUR

Somewhere in Europe and around 1851 an event was beginning to take place. It seems that there was to be the first International Tournament take place and another smaller, but very well organized tournament was to be offered as an "Open Tournament" to anyone who wished to play. While it was still in the planning stages, the committee received a post from someone who claimed he could beat most to the Masters who were expected to attend.

He further offered to pay a stake of 60£ to anyone who could beat him at a game of chess. However, should he win he would expect to be paid a stake of 50£. Also, should the game be a drawn game, he expected to be paid 25£ for his efforts. There was one final stipulation and that was that he was to play only masters, or those of equivalent abilities. Further, that it had to be a simultaneous match and he would choose his colors at the time of the match and that there had to be twelve, or more, participants.

The committee had never heard of the man, Reginald Thomas, but his offer of such high stakes was impressive. Prior to their answering his post, they solicited queries from several masters to find if they might be interested. The masters had little problem with the challenge as it could be easy money too win. It seems they too, had not heard of a player by that name.

The committee agreed to his terms, but they wanted the simultaneous match to take place before the main International tournament. Their reasoning was to use it as a drawing card and to allow the masters a chance to warm up before the main event.

Reginald Thomas brought along a second, but his role was to handle the financial aspects of the tournament. He also insisted that each player be seated at a table that was independent of others, so that the other players could not second guess his moves by observing another player's game while it was in progress.

It seemed odd to the committee when he chose his colors, because he chose to play black at the first table, white at the second table, black at the third table, and continued to alternate the color he played at each of the following tables. When the match began, he stood while his opponent played his opening move, and Reginald followed with his move. He then made the corresponding move for the black pieces. When this was completed, he moved to the next board, and so it went until he returned to the first board once again. In the end he drew six games, lost two, and won four. This resulted in his paying out 120£, bur winning 200£ for won games and 150£ for drawn games.

Over a celebration dinner following the simultaneous match, his second said."I didn't realize you were that accomplished at the game of chess."

"I'm not really an exceptional player."

"How was it then, that you did so well?"

He smiled as he said. "I played them against themselves."

Surprised by the answer, he said. "I'm not sure I understand."

"Well, when one of my opponents made a move, I repeated that move at the next table I played at. In the end I was only a paid messenger between twelve of the finest chess players in the world."

THE FASTEST CLOCKS

Any chess player can tell you that chess clocks are the fastest running clocks in the world. Before clocks it was common for a match game to go on for hours on end. Until the middle of the nineteenth Century, chess matches were played until they were over, regardless of how long a player took to analyze and make his moves.

The Macdonnell - La Bourdonnais match game often lasted all night. As either player could take as long as they liked, two hours per move happened as well. It was Howard Staunton's insistence that finally brought about the timing of chess games during matches. This would be the same man who designed our current chessmen used in tournament play today.

The first modern timed game method was to use an hourglass, and each player had to make 24 moves within two hours. Sand-glasses were some of the first timing devices tried, and before a tournament started each player would get a sand-glass. It was to be laid down on its side while the other player was making his, or her, moves.

Sometimes, inadvertently of course, one of them would get turned back up, but on the opposite end which of course started his sand going as if from the beginning, or at least earlier in the game. This only seemed to happen if one of them was running out of time.

Today's chess clock started its journey around 1880, and the better of them was invented in England by Thomas Bright Wilson. There was a great tournament in 1851 where the chess clock was used and it gave a much needed boost to the games. In 1852 a time limit of 20 minutes was introduced in a match between Horowitz and Lowenthal.

The better clock, invented by Mr. Wilson, was used in the London tournament in 1883. This clock had a dial indicating the number of moves made and a bell that rang after a set number of moves had been made. The first official use of chess clocks took place in the Paris tournament in 1867.

After the original breakthrough of timing a chess game, numerous clocks have found their way to the chess matches. In 1933-34 the first really modern chess clock was assembled by Curtis R. Wilson in Oakland California and it only used one clock movement. Today, 40 moves in two and a half hours, and 16 moves in every following hour are the acceptable method. Though time rates are often adjusted to a particular tournament in play.

THE KNIGHT SACRIFICE

When chess came to Europe from Persia, about the sixth century, it was played by Kings and his Royal courtesans. In a sense it was a game used to practice warfare on other Kingdoms. It was very popular and most Kings knew how to play the game, or at least had a basic knowledge of the game. History will tell you that the game has since changed a great deal, but it still carries the lessons of how to plan attacks, or to think strategically ahead of time.

When the Greek and Roman Kings were involved in a long-standing battle over the city of Troy, which was actually a battle over the woman known as Helen of Troy, a woman that each of the Kings desired to possess. The Greek King sent hundreds of men to their death in fighting this battle, and the battle lasted for ten years. Now, however, I'll tell you about a part of the story that most people know little about.

During the siege on Troy the Greek King's Generals came to him and complained, "Your Majesty, most of our soldiers have been killed trying to storm the castle walls. We've been fighting with them for ten years and still we have not captured the city of Troy. We cannot continue to sacrifice more men in this war."

The King was angry that his generals were questioning his orders, but he also knew there was some truth in their complaints.

Still, dismayed, he asked his Generals to wait a few days while he made his final decision. During which time they were well fed and nurtured back to health during their stay. They were also entertained while the King continued to worry about the problem. One morning he called his war council together, and even after all this time he asked, "What do you suggest we do?"

His Generals, and the war council wanted to call an end to the war, but they knew the King wanted the woman, Helen. Finally someone in the group made the suggestion.

"Your Majesty, why not consider leaving a gift for the Romans, then simply walk away.".

"A gift, you say?" What kind of soldier was this, why leave a gift and give up the battle as well? Still, he would hear him out.

"Aye, your Majesty. It is customary for the King to leave a King's horse as a sign that the battle is over. So, like in a game of chess, why not surprise them with a gift of a Sacrificed Horse?" A broad smile crossed his face as he saw the King thinking of what it was he'd suggested.

The King too, smiled as he understood the meaning of the 'Sacrificed Horse.' That very day he called on the artist, 'Opeues,' to build the horse. It was quickly assembled and when it was done, it was towed during the dark of night to the front gates of the castle walls of Troy and left there to be found at the following daybreak.

The next morning the Roman guards from Troy found the large wooden horse outside the city gates. It was inspected carefully, but not carefully enough. Still it was taken as an offer, and a sign that the Greek King had tired of battle.

Once everyone was satisfied that it was safe to accept the large wooden horse, and with no sign of the enemy in sight, even their ships were gone from the nearby port. The offering was pulled inside the city gates of Troy. Everyone was so happy that the siege of Troy had come to an end that they began to celebrate. By the end of the day every soldier inside the city walls was either sleeping, or had consumed too much to drink. In the early hours of the following morning, and while it was still dark, no one noticed that forty men came crawling out of the belly of the large wooden horse.

Those forty men simply opened the gates to the city of Troy and the remaining Greek army entered and enslaved everyone inside the city walls. They had captured the city by simply offering a sacrificial horse. This is an indication of how long ago the art of sacrificing a chess piece has turned a lost game into a won game.

A WIFE'S DILEMMA

As the story goes, it seems that in the tenth century an Arab Vizier, and ardent chess player, once got involved in a series of chess games of which a wager was expected. Considering himself a competent chess player, he started playing against a player of unknown strengths.

His wife, Dilaram, watched as he wagered, and game after game he lost, in the end he lost nearly all of his possessions. In one last attempt too win a game of chess against his opponent, he offered his wife as the prize to be had.

Horrified, at the possibility of leaving the game as someone else's woman, and understanding the game to some depth herself she watched the game more closely as it progressed. The game was played badly by the shaken Vizier and should have been lost, however, his wife, Dilaram, noticed a possibility of sacrificing his two Rooks for an ending that would give him the game.

She leaned over and whispered in her husband ear of her thoughts, he looked up at her, smiling, and after some further study, he did as she suggested. In the end he won the game, and saved his wife for himself.

THE AIR AROUND CHESS

There have been times that I've wondered how dangerous chess really is, this is a curiosity, and a feeling that comes over me from time to time. Such as the last time I visited the Café de la Régence in Paris. It happened as I roamed around the Café one evening in 1909 I could feel the presence of men past, and present. Perhaps I should help you understand these feelings I got by pointing a few places you might have been during your lifetime.

Places where you experienced certain feelings yourself, as if the air itself is charged in some manner. If you've ever seen a ghost, you will remember the feeling of your hair raising up on the back of your neck, knowing very well you could see the ghost and that the ghost was aware of your presence as well. Or, perhaps you can remember the quiet while walking through a graveyard when no one else was about. It is not just quiet. It is a deathly quiet. A quiet time not experienced elsewhere. If none of these, then maybe you've entered a monastery, or cathedral and could feel the presence of something not felt anywhere else. Perhaps not God like, but some kind of comforting presence.

Even going into someone's home where you felt the comfort and a knowledge you were welcome to stay. Being aware of those feelings let me tell you about the feelings I got as I walked about the playing rooms of the Régence on this one particular evening.

The weather outside was foul, and as I entered the Café the first thing I could smell was the dampness of wool overcoats, that and the permeating smell of cigar smoke. I did not have a game of chess arranged for this evening, I had just decided at the last moment to stop in and perhaps observe a game of two in progress. It is common to find several men standing around one table of another watching games as they are played. Sometimes making an observation out loud, then being shushed as kibitzing is still frowned upon, especially here in these sober surrounding. Well, not everyone was sober, just the mood at a few tables.

As I passed the favorite table that Paul Morphy had used when he played here, you could almost feel the mental despair hanging over the table, as if his last years were present around this very spot. Of course at the time he played here there may not have been any indication that he would succumb to mental disorder in the coming years, or was there? He died an odd death as I recall. He'd been out in the cold, then returned home to take a hot bath, and was found dead in the tub. Or so I'm led to believe. Other rumors have it that there was a woman behind hie demise, and this would not surprise me as it has happened to others before.

After experiencing the feeling I had around the Paul Morphy table, and out of curiosity I moved over to the table where William Steinitz liked to play chess when he was in the club. He too had a bad ending in life. He died poverty stricken and out of his mind.

The game that was currently in progress was being played poorly so I moved on. Next I went over to the table that Nelson Pillsbury always sat at.

Standing near the table and watching the two men silently battle each another for a commanding position on the board, I made it a point to try and feel the presence around the table. Perhaps I'm just more susceptible to these things, or just in this way of thinking. But, here too, there was something in the air. Immediately I recalled that Nelson was one of the stronger blind chess players. In fact just a few short years ago he had played several blindfold games here all at the same time. Let me think now it was. . . .Sixteen games at a time if I recall correctly. Oh yes, and he was playing two games of checkers and a few hands of Whist all at the same time. Phenomenal, just phenomenal. Of course in the end the mental strain was what many think killed him in the year 1906.

Another table was so enshrouded in cigar smoke that you would have thought there to be walls around it to keep the smoke close to the table. It reminded me of Lasker's smelly cigars. He smoked them and then blew the smoke at his opponent's face, unkind of course, but effective. It did keep spectators away from the table, I myself included.

Over the years I've tried talking to these kinds of mental chess giants, but it can't be done. Oh, don't misunderstand me, you can talk to them about chess, but nothing else. No, it's not that they won't talk about other things, they would if they could. They simply don't know about anything else, as their whole world is chess and only chess. They are like small islands among continents. They know they exist, but they are not sure of anything more than the world they inhabit.

After I left the club, I adjourned to my quarters. The following morning I took my clothing to a laundress nearby for a washing. As I passed them over to her, she looked at them, then sniffed them and said to me. "You've been to the Café Regernce."

"Yes, how did you know this?"

"Your clothes reek of the place."

THE CHESS BOOK

I was fortunate in the sense that I happened by the, Caxton's Press on that day in 1474. Fortunate because the second book ever printed in the English language was coming off the press that day. As each page was pulled from the inked plate of the press, it was being hung to dry on a line strung across one side of the room. I knew that from that point, that when the pages were dry they would be sewn together into a book titled. *"Game and the plays of chesses."* It turns out, that it was being translated from a French version of the same book. It had been written by a Friar, Jacobus de Cessolis in the last quarter of the thirteenth century.

I also learned, while in the print shop of William Caxton, that he himself was an avid chess player, and that he was already considering plans for a later edition of this same book, but it was to have many illustrations. However, the amount of work to be done to print that edition would require a great deal of effort on the part of the printer and his apprentices. It would involve many engravings for the illustrations, and perhaps a new press as well.

Still here I was, witnessing the first book of chess to be printed, and the second book to be printed in the English language.

THE KING IS GONE

Purssell's, a chess club of some years standing, was often found to be a haven for chess players of any age group. Those who attended this unique establishment often fled from those who were average basic wood pushers. To come into contact with world Grandmasters, and this story comes from that time, now long since past.

Two gentlemen, both well along in their years, were playing chess late one evening. They were tired and each was trying to stay awake long enough to make their next move, they simply didn't want the day to end. Mr. Adams had opened with the King's Gambit, but Mr. Brown was fighting his way through the crowded center of the board.

Mr. Adams saw his chance to castle, and did so on the King's side. However, in his careless manner, accidently brushed his King off the board and it fell to the floor, landing amid a small collection of other debris on the floor and it went unnoticed by himself and a good many others who were close by.

Mr. Brown, who had been planning to move his King's Bishop off the original square so that he too could castle, figured he could move the Bishop to the Queen's Bishop four square and put his opponent in check at the same time.

After Mr. Adams had settled down with his last move completed, Mr. Brown was quick to move the Bishop as planned, and after removing his fingers from the piece, and without looking closely at the board, he said. "Check."

Except that when he, and Mr. Adams looked at the board, there was no King to put in check, it had vanished. After a few moments, Mr. Adams found his King on the floor and placed it in check.

This of course brings the question of doing this, as you cannot move your King into check

THE CHOIR BOY

I had been standing in an archway trying to stay out of the sudden downpour of rain, and waiting for it to ease off. While I stood there, hurrying up the steps came an old gentleman, who, in passing, caught my eye. He smiled and said. "Come inside with me, it is warmer and dry. You can wait until the rain lets up."

I knew I was just outside the church's chapel and saw no reason not to accept his invitation, so I nodded my agreement and followed him inside. As he moved up the center aisle, I followed fairly close behind. Then abruptly he stopped, turned to look around, and seemed disappointed. However, there was a young lad sitting on the bench close to our end, and just beyond him I could see several chess boards resting on the top of the bench.

He asked the young boy. "Where are the others?"

"They have not arrived yet, Sir."

"I was looking for a game before the choir started."

The boy, seemed hesitant, but offered. "I can play chess a bit, Sir. If you like I can get the pieces so we can play while we wait."

The old man seemed reluctant to play this very young boy, but nodded his accent, and the boy rushed off.

While he was gone, the old man explained the situation to me. "I am their musician, but early each morning, before Choir practice, most of the lads play chess here on the benches. Some of them are quite good, but this young lad, though a choir boy, I've not seen him play before."

When the boy returned, he and the musician set up the pieces and began to play a game of chess. At first the musician laughed at how the youngster played the game. Within a few more moves he began to get irritated at his constant loss of pieces. By now others had arrived and gathered around. Even from where I stood, they were beginning to crowd the aisle and fill in behind the adjoining pews. Everyone was surprised at the lad of ten, and at how well he was playing the game.

I learned that In conversations around the church in the following days, others were becoming aware of the choir boy at the church. It seems he was obtaining quite a following because of his chess ability. This was the beginning for Philidor, but when he left the Choir at age fourteen, he was known to be the best chess player in the land.

As is common for older men, when they lose a chess game to a youngster, they can secretly nurture an anger at themselves for having lost to such a young player. I myself am included in this group. We become forgetful.

E2 - E4

In 1962 Arthur M. Stevens knew he was on to something big, and something he felt was odd. He had an extensive collection of chess games. All played by the masters. A collection. That had taken him fourteen years to accumulate, was telling him something important. This collection of material was now filling one hundred and twenty-six file drawers and was at the time stored in a rickety old garage.

He had designed and had a printer print special forms that he had designed and that he ordered by the thousands. The forms were depicting chess moves one after the other and with the percentage of possible wins in each game. He began working fifteen hours a day to work his way through his collection, and to record every game available to him at the time.

Then, on January 27, 1967 he announced to the world that he knew something that no other man had known before. He proclaimed that when White moves Pawn to King's four, e2-e4, he wins 59.1% of his games. His book, 'The Blue Book of Winning Chess' can still be found, though it was published in 1969 - SBN 489-07362-9 and is still one of the most comprehensive studies of this kind.

LOOK WHO'S HERE

Alexander Alehkine had once been asked to speak at a
public function, began telling the audience about a dream
he'd had the night before. He said, "I dreamed I'd died
and gone to heaven, and on my arrival St. Peter met me
at the gate. As he looked me over, he enquired as to
whom I was. "I answered. I am Alehkine, the greatest
chess champion of the world. "

But, St. Peter informed me, "Chess players are not
allowed in Heaven."

I was greatly dismayed, of course. However, before
turning back I took a quick look around, and behold I
saw before me my old friend, Bofolubov. I drew St.
Peter's attention to him and said. "He's a chess player."

St. Peter shook his head slowly and replied, "He only
thinks he's a chess player."

TOUCH IF YOU DARE

This was an interesting new rule that came into play
about the year of 1497. It seems that the game of playing
chess for stakes in the Middle ages, necessitated some
stricter rules. This rule is still the same one we use today,
and it can actually help a player. If he or she uses it to
their advantage. Even if it is only self imposed, and does
not necessarily apply to one's opponent.

The reasoning behind this line of thinking, is that it
makes a player think more in depth about the game in
front of him before making a commitment. The touching
a piece of either player's, yours or theirs, and then
changing your mind about the upcoming play, you have
inadvertently telegraphed to the opposing player what the
potential future might hold.

With this information, an opponent can block, or re-
enforce that area of the board. Still, at the same time, you
could use this kind of ploy to mislead an opponent into
thinking you are considering moving a certain piece
when you almost touch it, but not moving it, and thereby
cause him, or her, into an erroneous way of thinking.

NOW, WHERE TO?

Emanuel Lasker had made the decision to go to Paris to play chess at the famous club, Café de la Regence. When he arrived there his first evening, he became so deeply involved in playing a game of chess, that he played well into the early morning hours. After he left the Café, he couldn't remember how to get back to the Inn where he had previously rented a room, nor could he remember the location it was in, within the city.

Someone Lasker had met during the evenings chess games came across him as he wandered about and learned of his plight. The gentleman who found him took pity on him, and then offered to let Lasker stay at his home while he continued looking for the Inn where he had reserved rooms for his stay. Finally, in desperation, Lasker sent a telegram to a friend in London asking him where it was that he had made his reservations before he'd left home. However, in his haste he forgot to tell his friend where to send the answer. The friend answered his request as soon as he could, except he had to send the reply to the Inn where Lasker had booked his room, all because he didn't know where Lasker was waiting to hear from him.

Lasker spent most of the next day methodically searching the city for the Inn, and eventually he found it. When he entered the building, the woman who was in charge, handed him a telegram which told him where he was staying.

I DON'T KNOW HOW TO PLAY

I don't recall the year, but at the Café de la Régence in Paris, there was a man who spent several years attending the club, ten years at least. Upon his arrival each day, he would take his coffee and roam the room looking over the shoulders at games in play. He never kibitzed, and rarely spoke to anyone, other than one of the waiters who might be attending the player's needs. He just wandered around and watched the games as they progressed. He was often offered a seat at a table and to take part in a game of chess, but he always refused to play.

It was during a local tournament, and as this man was watching the deciding moves in a game, that a problem arose as to a chess rule. The two gentlemen seated at the board looked up at the man in question, and asked. "You, Sir. What are your findings in this matter?"

Frustrated, and much to his dislike, he replied. "Monsieur, I don't know how to play the game, nor do I know the name of the pieces."

Both men were astonished. One of them said. "You have been coming here for years on end, watching thousands of games in play, and you don't know how to play chess?"

"Oui, Monsieur."

"Pray tell, dear fellow, why do you come here then?"

After taking a sip of his coffee, he said. "I am a married man and I don't want to go home."

THE MAHARAJA'S VIZIER

Some who traveled with us in this caravan, thought of me as a wealthy merchant. In reality I had arranged my passage with the owner of this caravan which was now traveling across the sands of time. I had not paid a fee to travel with this band of tradesmen, but had agreed to keep notes of what merchandise was most sought after in the markets of the villages and cities as we moved across this wide world. My records would then allow the owner to plan his next caravan's trip and what wares his group would carry for markets along the way.

As we traveled I soon learned that, Rukmin, the head man of our caravan was almost always sought out so as to meet with the heads of the royal courts along our journey. It was done in this manner so the ministers of his, or her, majesty could have first picks of the items our caravan carried along the way.

On one of these long, hot and dusty day we stopped in a valley much richer in vegetation than I would have expected for this part of the world. We were blessed with a small river nearby and apparently the local villagers had some knowledge of irrigation as the area had been turned into a wonderful spectacle of color. Our group began to settle into a camp area near the river, when an emissary from the Rajah's court arrived to welcome us.

As he spoke to Rukmin, he saw me standing nearby. I knew he was asking about me because Rukmin looked my way and smiled.

After the court's emissary left our encampment, Rukmin came to me and explained. "You and I are to enjoy a meal with his majesty this evening. He is Maharajah Balhait and a very powerful man."

As I was not always invited to attend these kinds of events, I had to ask. "How is it that I'm to go with you?"

"The man who spoke with me about this evening noticed the clothing you wear and became curious about you. When I explained, you were a foreigner from a far country he mentioned there might be someone in the Maharajah's court would like to speak to you."

Because I dress in a button up shirts and trousers, I do attract attention. The normally used mode of dress while traveling with a caravan is in flowing robes which let the air flow around your body and allow some coolness, whereas mine did not.

In my curious response I said. "Who in the Rajah's court would want to talk with me?"

He smiled, but only replied. "I have no idea who that might be, but I would advise you not to refuse the invitation."

*   *   *

That evening as we supped on a meal of great varieties and proportions and accompanied by unusual wines, a man came from behind me and asked if I might remain

47

behind when the rest of our group left to return to our encampment. At the man's question my eyes met those of Rukmin, who was at my left and I saw his head nod a yes to me. I in turn agreed to stay later and the man disappeared.

As our main party prepared to leave, the same man came again to me, bowed, then indicated the direction I was to follow. We walked outside into a magnificent courtyard which had flowers and plants I've not seen anywhere before. I can only tell you're the fragrance was astounding. I was almost overwhelmed in the perfumed air after traveling the barren desert. Just a short distance away from the doorway from which we had come, my guide stopped at another door, he knocked lightly, then motioned for me to enter.

The room was large, and well lighted from openings that would be hard to cover in cooler weather. Also, in view across the room from where I stood, I could see a large-tiled patio. A man dressed in rich clothing, and dyed in colors that were astounding to the eye. I approached as his hand beckoned for my own, and he said.

"I am the Maharajah's Vizier, Sissa."

I did not know what position this might be in this court at the time, but I knew it was an important level of the Rajah staff. A man who held a minister's position is always one of power. I simply said, "I am Donald, from across the seas."

"Would you care for some wine?"

I had, had quite a bit of wine already, but I agreed to his suggestion to be polite as Rukmin had warned me against refusal at invitations. "Yes, of course I would enjoy some wine with you."

As I followed him out toward the patio we passed by something that immediately caught my eye, and I mentioned it without calling it by the name I knew of. "This is an impressive item you have here." I said as I pointed to it on a low table.

His eyes danced with excitement as he asked. "Do you know of games and puzzles?"

Well, I knew of this game and the puzzles it brings to men's minds, but I did not say this. Instead I said. "Yes, I am familiar with games and puzzles."

"Wonderful. That is exactly why I wanted to speak to you this evening. You see, I Have just returned from other lands. I was seeking knowledge of a game the Rajah wanted to use to teach others the finer arts of war and the way to think ahead. To develop one's foresight and diligence. I have labored many hours in my search for the understanding of its intricacies and would value your impression of the game."

Being from another world, so to speak, I was well aware of the game, but I did not let him know that. Instead I asked for his explanation and understanding of the game.

He told me of the pieces and how they were to move about the board, and though they did not look like anything we use today, I understood that the meaning of the Foot soldiers, Elephants, vizier, Chariots, and Horses.

It did not take long for me to understand which ones were like our Pawns and Rooks, in a sense a limited Queen, also with knights and the like. He explained the game could be played with two players, or four as needed. Whichever was required for an evening's entertainment. He was equally amazed at my grasping the game so quickly as he explained it to me, and we began to play a few games.

It was near morning before we retired for what was left of the night and I found I was expected to be a guest on the royal grounds until the caravan left to continue its journey.

During the games, the following night, I took a chance and made a few suggestions to the Vizier about how he might consider changing his opening moves. I explained how he could grab control of the battlefield early and so control the game before him and his opponent. He thought me a brilliant man, whereas I have the knowledge of how to play a good game, although I am not one of high standing in that realm. However, to a man new to the game, and one who thought of his grasp of it, I seemed an astounding player.

After another night of playing this new game he explained to me how he had to show the Maharajah his newly acquired knowledge and asked.

"Would you tell me what you think of this game, and I need to know it without a falsehood?"

I sat quietly for a few moments, gathering my thoughts before I spoke. "I think you have before you, a game that will stand the test of time for centuries to come. Your name will be remembered for all time in the court."

He smiled broadly, "Do you really feel this way about this game?"

"Without a doubt."

I had enjoyed my stay on the royal grounds as I was able to bathe, have my clothes washed, get my beard trimmed and eat fabulous meals. However, back with the caravan, and just as we were about to leave the banks of the river, the same man who had approached me at the first dinner, came again to me. He handed me a leather pouch just as I was mounting my camel. He bowed deeply, then turned and walked away without a word. As we settled into our trek, I looked inside the pouch and found to my delight, several gold coins.

BLIND MAN'S CHESS

As I recall it was while I was in Damascus about 1331, or so, that I came across an unusual chess situation. Though I was just an observer I was close enough to hear the words being spoken, still my language skills were minimal for the local dialect. As I watched the game in play I found it odd that the player closest to me played the game in a skillful manner, but he seemed to touch the pieces on occasion. As if he was adjusting them on a continual basis, but he wasn't.

I watched a few minutes longer, then leaned close to the ear of the man I'd come with and whispered, "Shamsaddin." As I spoke, I pointed with my fingers to one of the players. "He plays the game in an odd manner, as if he is reassuring the pieces of their role in the game." I had spoken quietly so as not to disturb the game, and when I'd finished I could see a smile cross Shamsaddin's face.

Slowly he turned to me and said, "The man is blind as a bat. He cannot see the pieces. He touches them occasionally to be certain his memory is correct. Anyone who plays chess with him does not mind his game manners."

I was astounded by what he'd said to me. Could this be true, was the man actually blind? I couldn't resist so I asked. "You're telling me he actually cannot see the game in front of him?"

Again he smiled, then turned to the game and called out. "al-Ajami, show us how the game has taken place, you see we came late and missed a few of the moves."

When the man turned toward us, I no longer questioned his blindness. His eyes were dark as well as deeply sunken into his head. He looked, but not quite at us, just in our direction. He asked. "Who is it that speaks?"

"It is I, Shamsaddin."

His head turned slightly at the sound of the voice and now he faced us directly. "Ahhh, my friend Shamsaddin. You shall see the game as it was played."Without looking back at the board al-Ajami picked up each piece one at a time, and in the reverse order of play and put them back on the squares they had previously been on. He did this until all of the chess pieces were back on their original squares. Once done with this, he said. "This is how the game took place."

He then proceeded to make each move one at a time, his and his opponents, until he had the game back to its current state of play. Then he turned to his opponent and said. "Is this not correct my friend?"

The man sitting across from him replied. "It is it as you say."

THE FIRST MASTER

In the ninth century, aL-Adli was the strongest chess player to be found. No one could beat him at the game. This ability eventually led him to write the first book about the technicalities of the game. He wanted other players to get better at the game so he would have some competition. As he played different opponents, he would keep notes about the game and the errors of the game. His notes would then be added to his book. This same book found its way into the hands of a tenth century player, also a chess master and also unbeatable. He had played so many individuals that he began the first classifications of chess players. The best he labeled as "Grandees." They had to be able too mentally play ten moves ahead.

The next was the. "Proximes." This player had to be able win two out of ten games from a Grandee with odds of a Pawn to retain his title.

The next level, the third, had to do the same, but with odds of Bishop. The fourth level was given odds of a Knight. The fifth level had odds of a Rook.

Other masters, or Grandees, such as Alessandro Salvio, Giucio Poleria, and Giacchino Greco all kept precise notes and records of their games.

However, they had no intention of writing books, or even sharing their findings with the general chess public. Instead they sold their information to those of substance who had the means to spend huge amounts of money for such information. The intention being, of course, to become much better players themselves.

THE OPENINGS

The newer player to the game of chess rarely thinks of how may ways he could start to play a game of chess. Even as your chess knowledge expands it can be overwhelming to learn how many possibilities there are in a game of this magnitude. It seems simple enough to make an opening, and you can use any method you like. Most of us have our favorite openings, and in this generation the more favored are the Queen's Gambit, the King's Gambit, and the, Evans' Gambit is still used a great deal. Even the standard P-K4 / e2 - e4 opening is used to see where the game goes from this point. However, you know that just the Pawns alone offer sixteen different possibilities. I read the number somewhere that mathematics tell us there are 318,979,655,000 variations just in openings. Yet by the time you get to the tenth move, you are at a staggering 169,518,829,100,544.000,000,000,000 plus or minus a few million.

When you consider this amount of opening potential, can you imagine the amount of mental capacity a blindfold chess player needs to carry on several games at once. If you imagine an average game lasting twenty-five moves and the blindfold player is playing ten games, he may have to remember two hundred and fifty moves all at the same time. And when you think about the potential of playing thirty or forty games at the same time, the number of moves one has to keep in his, or her, head is well beyond most of mankind's ability.

Is it any wonder why some of those who were able to do this died of mental exhaustion?

If my understanding is correct, when it is their turn to make the next move, these blindfold chess players don't even have to go over the moves they've made during a game with each opponent, they remember the exact position of the pieces and make their move without hesitation. Then they move onto the next game in play.

HENRY BLACKBURNE

Henry could be found frequently as a chess player at the chess club, 'Purssell's, in London. It was on one of those days when he arrived to play, and was about to start a game of chess with an older man, a man who was known to lose his temper quickly. He was one who always played chess by the rules and insisted that everyone else did the same. Those who were aware of this man's idiosyncracies, also knew he could not take a joke no matter how simple.

Henry, not someone to let this kind of information get by him, watched the old man make his first move on the board. The old man moved P-K3 / E2-4, and after he removed his fingers from the piece, Henry said. "Ahhh, now I resign." The old man, who was not someone to trifle with, said. "Alright. That's one game for me." Henry, knowing there was no way to convince the old man it had been a joke, let the game be recorded in the club's history. At the time this was the shortest chess game on record.

Henry Blackburne was the man who made the French Legal's Mate popular. Though, because of him, it became known more as, "The black death," or, "The Blackburne trap." It is a good opening to use against a greedy player as it employees a Queen sacrifice.

Henry was also a strong believer in the use of scotch whisky. He was known to become quite angry when he drank too much, and often took his anger out on his opponents.

During the Hastings match in 1895, Henry Blackburne drank a case of scotch whisky during the first six rounds of play.

To say Henry was a man of chess, may be an understatement. He was known to play 4000 games of chess a year, or more.

NAPOLEON BONAPARTE

We know Napoleon was an avid chess player, he played almost every day, but he was not a good chess player. When he lost a game of chess, he became moody and angry, he simply wasn't a good loser. He did not have chess savvy, he could play but he either refused to learn how to make proper opening, or no one would take a chance on telling him that he needed to learn how to improve his game. His mood swings were known to be dangerous if you were on his bad side, so those in his close circle were wary of advising him on strategy of any kind.

Such was the case when Napoleon heard about the Duke, 'Duc d'Enghien' as being rebellious in matters not conducive to Napoleon's way of thinking. Though he had sent for the Duke, and though Napoleon was still non committal, the Duke was to be put to death. Napoleons' wife, Josephine heard about it before it took place and she, and her lady in waiting, Contesse Claire de Remusat' went to Napoleon's quarters to speak to him about sparing the young man's life. However, Napoleon was playing chess at the time, and the two women interrupted his game. Josephine pleaded for the Duke's life, but to no avail. Napoleon looked up from the game before him and said. "Stop referring to this matter. Now, it is settled." The Duke, was given a trail, but it seemed to be a poor representation of one, and he was still put to death. The cruel, vain attitude of Napoleon was further enhanced.

At the chess board it was common for him to sweep the men from the board, or to move pieces to squares not available to them. As a believer in the 'Calvary' he favored his Knights, however he moved them to suit his need, even if the rules were such that the Knights couldn't move the way he moved them. The proper way to play chess by using proven openings, just never came to his mind. He was, in a sense, blind to advancing his game ability. His mind was closed on the subject and it stayed that way, even when he was finally abolished from France by those who seized power and they sent him into exile, living out his remaining years on the Island of St. Helena.

THE WAY THINGS ARE

This is a written work from the middle ages, believably by a Franciscan Friar, John of Waleys. It is a comparison of the game of chess to that of life. One of the things I liked in reading what little information there is, was where it is said. "When the pieces are placed in a bag, the King often lies at the bottom and is no better than a Pawn. Much the same way as in life after death. As in death all men are equal regardless of the station they held in life."

Part of the explanation of how the chess pieces move, was explained as follows. The King moves and captures in any direction. He can do this because his will is law. The Queen can move any direction aslant, because women are greedy and can change their minds to achieve their needs. The Bishops move obliquely, because nearly every Bishop is corrupt and misuses his power. The Knights move partially obliquely and straight which is common with his extortions and wrongdoings. The Rooks move is always straight because he represents justice. The Pawn moves straight until he captures, which is similar to life in his quest for wealth and rank.

NOW here is another newer rendition of the same idea.

Pawns

These are the foot soldiers and they do the bidding of the King and Queen. Much like our fire and police departments of today. These pieces get moved on the board according to the whims of the King and of the Queen's needs, or perhaps to help the Bishops as needed.

The King and Queen Pawns in the center, are the ones who open the drawbridge to allow passage of the Bishops, and the royal family as needed. Sometimes they may jump out two squares in the beginning so that they can get better control of those assembling around the end of the drawbridge. The other Pawns act only when ordered to do so, more often to attack an enemy who is close to the castle walls.

Though in the end game, or the end of the war, a Pawn may make a dash for the other kingdoms walls, and if he gets inside safely, his King will reward him. He can become any member of the royal family, except that of a King. He can take on a disguise as a Queen and have the same power, or he can become a Bishop or a Knight. Pawns are also used to protect others on the battlefield like that of a body guard.

Bishops

In times of old, the Bishops were the more powerful of the church's members. Bishops were always available to advise the King, or Queen. They would tell the Royal family what was right and wrong, or what they should consider doing for the welfare of the Kingdom.

Both the King and the Queen, in case they needed guidance, kept their own personal Bishop nearby. A Bishop, when leaving the safety of his home square within the castle walls, can look ahead, and to both sides. This ability gives him the same influence as three Pawns.

A Bishop kept behind the castle walls cannot advise the King or Queen about what is going on outside. The Bishops need to get out among the soldiers so they can see what is happening. Bishops often point out a good place for the Queen to go shopping, she listens to her Bishops' advice, and considers the Knights ability to protect her on some of her outings. Bishops are good pieces to have in your corner of the world.

Knights

Though they work for the King and Queen, the Knights were often found doing favors for the Bishops as well. When the King, the Queen, or a Bishop needs information from some distant outpost on the chessboard, they may send a Knight to investigate.

A knight, which, when placed on the edge of the chessboard, is in a sense, sitting in a corral. On the edge the board, a Knight's moves are cut in half. In the center of the board a Knight can move to eight different locations, on the edge he can move to four. The Knight, in the Staunton pattern resembles a horse, has the power of three good Pawns. That is, the Knight, with a helmet on, can see straight ahead, the horse does not see straight ahead, but can see in two other directions at the same time.

Knights, because they can jump around the battlefield so easily, may find themselves in a position where they can attack, two, three, or perhaps even four pieces at one time. This is known as a fork, it is a powerful position because all of the pieces under attack, cannot scurry to safety, one will be taken. If the piece the Knight is after is of greater value than himself, a Knight might sacrifice his own safety to make the capture. Knights can protect other pieces on the board, or they can capture a threatening enemy.

Rooks

These pieces are more powerful when they are in a good position. Yet, in most games, they are kept behind the Kingdom's wall of soldiers, often until the final battle takes place. A Rook, when well placed on the chessboard, can defend in four directions a the same time. Think of the Rook as a castle tower around which can be moved. Inside the tower are four men armed with crossbows that can shoot long distances. Each of them looking out an open window and ready to shoot whatever enemy comes within range. Another man stands on top of the tower, his job, because he is higher, is to look around constantly to see if he can find an enemy to shoot at in the distance. So, the Rook is worth five Pawns.

Kings

The King sits at home most of the time, though his duties take place in several different ways. Among other things, he is kept there to arrange for the well being of his troops in the field. He looks after the affairs of his people, he arranges for his farmers to work their fields in ways that produce larger crops. These crops help feed everyone in the land. He deals with other kings when he can, or to attack other kingdoms when needed, or to protect his own kingdom if attacked. Sometimes, in the final battle, a King may go out to help his troops, but not unless they need him. The King has no Pawn power, because he is the King and cannot be replaced.

Queens

She is the most powerful person in the Kingdom. This is because of her many duties. She looks after the Kings well being. She sees that he receives his meals, his clothing and moral support.

Pay attention to what the Queen is doing at all times, what may seem to be a shopping trip to the other Queens' mall, may really be to take over the other Queens home for herself. Perhaps she takes a fancy to the other Queens Bishops, or a Knight or two, and she takes them home with her. Odds are she will only throw them into a dungeon, but she will have them if she can get them for nothing.

Sometimes it will seem as if the Queen is actually ruling the Kingdom, but keep in mind, she can be captured. Never make the Queen angry, she can throw you out into battle, and this is not a place to be without someone looking after your safety. The Queen has a value of nine Pawns. When at center board, she can move eight different directions, and she is taller than most others so she can see over their heads and she normally understands what they are doing at all times.

THE CHESS COACH

Some would say this is one of the most critical paths to follow in the game of chess. Teaching chess simply has to be done correctly. Over the centuries there have been literally thousands of us who under took this realm of the chess world. To those of us who do this, it is always rewarding in some manner. Whether it is the observing of a person's as they find new ways of thinking and the mental expanding of that thinking as it makes its way into their everyday life. To show each student a way of escaping the everyday hum drum of their lives, and to explore a world of mentality they had not thought possible. And yes, even the teacher who understands they may have instilled a fever, of sorts.

There are those who may think they would like to teach this game to others, but don't follow up on this line of thinking because they think their chess rating is not high enough to qualify them in the ways of the chess world. Actually, quite often the opposite is true. I have found the best teachers of chess only have a rating of around 1100 to 1300.

Any thing over that and often those who attempt to teach this game to new students are simply mentally too deep into the game to teach the basics needed. They are simply to far advanced in the game to go back and spend time on the basics. In their minds they think you should already know this stuff.

It is the advancing player needs those whose mind's dwells in the 1800 to 2200 rating range, but not beginners.

Over time a great number of us who begin to teach chess to new players have read numerous methods others have used to teach the game. Still, most of us develop our own curriculum through trial and error, find what works best for our students.

There is an old saying that you can teach someone how the chess pieces move within thirty minutes, and that is often the case. I have found that on average it takes about one hundred and twenty hours to teach a good basic foundation on how to play, and what to look for during the game. Is this enough just for the basics? I know not? It will vary from student to student.

One thing that drives a teacher of chess to exasperation is when the student who may know better, but makes an irregular opening. And as their teacher says to them. "You shouldn't open like that. An irregular opening like that will cost you the game."

The frustration comes with an answer like. "Why not?"

It is simply that you have to learn how to play chess before you can learn why you cannot open in strange ways. And yes, there are those who will argue this point.

Still, good solid openings are a proven point through history.

One thing I have found is that when children learn to play chess their scholastic grade levels increase for the better as they learn how to adapt to the method of planning ahead, also as their self confidence grows. They quickly learn that with a slight movement of the hand they can become giants. There is a good book presently available that can help guide the chess teacher. "The Chess Coach."

CORPORATE CHESS

I was to meet a friend of mine, Charles Morgan, in his
office late one morning, and I was made aware that he
wanted to show me something, then we were going to an
early lunch. When I arrived at Chuck's office, his
secretary said to go right in, as I was expected. I have to
tell you a bit of background here so you'll have a clearer
picture of the situation. You see, Chuck is a high-ranking
official within his company and his office is on one
corner of the top floor. It also overlooks the employee
parking lot between his wing of the building and that of
another top officer of the company who is across the
parking lot, and also on the top floor of the other wing.
The building is of a "U" shape and the two men can look
across to see each others office.

I knocked softly at his door, then entered to find him
with a cup of coffee in his hand, and looking down at the
parking lot. He glanced my way, then waved me over to
his side as he said. "You want a cup of coffee?"

"No, thanks."

Then he turned back to the window and said. "Look
down there and give me your opinion."

I looked down toward the parking lot, but drew a blank
as to what he wanted my thoughts on. "What?"I replied.

"The blue Ford that is parked on f3."

Bewildered, I looked for a blue Ford, and when I found it, the whole parking lot took on a different appearance as well. There was a complete section that did not have cars parked in it. Well there were some, but to the casual observer, they would have just been parked in those spaces randomly. However, to a chess player the parking lot came into focus as a giant chessboard. Not the whole parking lot of course, just a big chunk of the central area, and this area had much wider white lines on the outside edges. I also found that the cars on one side of the parking area were more blues and greys, whereas the cars on this side ran toward browns and blacks.

"Are you kidding me? You and someone else plays chess with your employees cars?"

"Hmm . . . Oh. Yes, with Bill Bowers, over there." He nodded his head across the way, and my gaze took in another man directly across from us, he too drinking coffee and looking down at the parking lot. "We have a parking schedule posted each afternoon and the employees check it to see where they are to park tomorrow. They always park where they are given an assigned number because it is some of the best parking we have available for access to the building."

He looked a few minuets longer, then consulted a chart on his desk top. After a brief moment he called his secretary and said. "Miriam. Would you have Mr. Stone park in g4, tomorrow?"

When he came back to the window, he said. "That'll pin the blue Ford."

I had to ask. "How long does it take to play a game?"

"Well . . . it varies. Longer than playing across the board of course. Sometimes weeks are involved. It's when someone is off sick that it gets really complicated."

THE DEATH OF A KING

I'm a traveling man, but not one of great wealth. Some would say I'm a gambler. You see I pay my way by playing chess for stakes, a wager if you will. When I enter a new towne or village of substantial size, I stay only at the better established men's clubs, or Inns where the more affluent are found to reside during their travels.

While there, and generally after a noon meal, I will often set up a chess board on my table, and place upon it a chess problem to be solved. Most of the time I will use a problem that needs only a single move to complete the checkmate. I do this because I do not want to make it too hard for another chess player to solve the problem within a short time. It is, after all, a gimmick to entice a passerby into playing a game.

Chess players cannot resist stopping by to observe a game in process. So when a possible player stops to have a look, I will sit, as if pondering what can I possibly do to make the correct move. Perhaps even reaching for the wrong piece to move, then putting it back from whence it came.

Even sighing at my frustration with the problem at hand. As a rule what happens is the onlooker will make a remark that leads to the solution. Such as. "If you move the Knight here, the game will be yours." A quick pointing of the fingers to indicate the required square for the Knight to reside upon.

I then, look up at them, as if in astonishment, and say. "Oh, you know something of this game?"

Egotism almost always carries a price tag of some kind. But more often than not my prospective player will reply will be along these, or of a similar line. "Well . . . Yes. I have some k knowledge of the game."

I will follow with some kind of invitation to join me. Such as, "Perhaps, if you've the time, you could assist me in bettering my understanding of how to play a proper game."

If there is some hesitation, but a chance they might sit down for a game, I'll offer. "I could use a good Brandy while we play, and of course I could purchase one for yourself as well."

When they do sit to play chess with me, and as we sip our drinks, I'll add a comment such as. "If I lose, I'll by the next round as well." If they accept this offer, they are committed to playing for a stake. Of course I'll lose and purchase the next drink for both of us. At some point they will lose, and of course will feel as if they have to purchase our next drink. Still, I try to drink moderately so that I can keep my wits about me. By the time my opponents have had two or three drinks they are quite loosened up, and much more susceptible.

Then I might say. "Perhaps we could play for a small wager instead of a drink. I'm getting tipsy and cannot play a proper game against such a worthy opponent?"

Generally by this time the player across from me has the notion they are winning most games handily and will readily accept such an offer. I will lose a game, or, if the evening is still young, I might lose two games in a row. However, I will then say. "It is growing late and I must get some rest. Perhaps, if you're willing, we could play for a larger final stake?"

Invariably the first thing they will ask, is. "How large a wager?"

I do not want to frighten them away now, so I say. "You can most likely afford more than I, a poor traveling man." If they offer a small sum as a wager. I may say. "Ahh . . . I would have expected more than a pittance from a man of your wealth."

They know they have been winning many games, and will most often offer a large stake. Of course the game will be tedious and close at every move. Still, somehow I will pull a winning combination at the last moment. Gather up the prize and adjourn for the evening.

On occasion a player will ask for one more game before I retire, and depending on their capabilities, I may agree, that is if the stake is high enough. Most of the time they will want to play for double the stakes of the last game. Expecting to get back what they may have already lost. Usually a costly error on their part. I almost always find myself twice as well off.

There was a time when I found myself in quite a self-imposed predicament because of my attitude while playing chess in this manner. I'd been playing chess in the south of France, and doing quite well.

Then I passed through Navarra to the South, and into the Kingdom of Castile. I had spent one night just across the border, and intended to travel deeper into the country the next day. Doing so, I found a busy establishment that catered to the more affluent travelers, and had come across a chess game in play during lunch. The game was between two elderly gentlemen. As you are aware, kibitzers are always found around games of chess, and I was no different in this realm. I made positive comments about how well they seemed to play the game of chess. This of course opened the opportunity to play chess with them as well. Of course this would be for stakes.

I'd been here nearly a fortnight playing chess during the days, and quite often during the evenings as well. One fine and profitable afternoon and while deep into a game, and while I was pondering my next move, others who were but watching the game in play, suddenly began making a commotion about something going on outside.

With my thoughts distracted I asked. "What is all the fuss about, gentlemen?"

Whereupon they parted a bit so I could see between them. What I observed was a very large, very ornate coach drawn by six beautiful Grays, the whole of it coming to a stop in front of the establishment in which we were all staying. Shortly a uniformed coachman entered the doors, looked quickly around the room, then came directly to our table. He looked at me as he said.

"Are you the chess player?"

Surprised, I said. "We are both chess players." My hand indicating the gentleman sitting across from myself as well.

"The one from England?"

"Yes. I am Ricardus, of English blood."

"His Majesty, King Peter of Castile wishes your attendance to play chess."

I was dumb struck. "The King wishes to play chess with me?"

"Gather your things. The King has sent his carriage for you."

I could see the carriage, so I don't know why he bothered to tell me this, but I knew I was going to the castle to play chess. No matter what else I might think.

I took only a short time to assembled my things, and to my surprise, on my leaving the premises, there was no mention of my debt while staying at the Inn. I can only suppose they were surprised, or in fear of my future.

The coach ride was fairly comfortable, but had I been riding in the normal carriage across this land, the trip would have been quite bumpy. I guess when you are a King, your carriages are much better built.

Arriving at the castle, I was met by a man dressed in robes that showed he was a man of means, and one who no doubt had a prominent position in the Kings counsel. He spoke to me as I departed the carriage. "I am, Jonathan. The Kings minister. Thank you for coming."

As if I had a choice in the matter. "I sir, am honored that the King wishes to play chess with me."

"Today you will rest. Perhaps in the morning the King will have time to play chess?"

He led me to my rooms, and I must say they were well appointed. The four poster bed, was larger than any I have ever seen before, let alone sleep in. I'd only been in my room a few brief moments when Jonathan returned with a manservant. I was to learn that he was to attend to my every wish, well at least as best he could. That evening I had quite a good hot bath in a large tub. The tub appeared to be carved from solid stone, I think, perhaps of Marble. My meal was delivered to my quarters and I dined on items I've never tasted before, but that look forward to experiencing again.

Later, with nothing else to do, I roamed freely within the castle walls. In doing so I came across a guarded door high in a tower and at the far end of the castle. I looked at the guard, and asked.

"What is it you have to guard in this isolated part of the castle?" He did not even blink an eye, nor did he answer me. To learn the answer I knew I would have to ask Jonathan.

The early next afternoon Jonathan came for me. When we arrived at our destination, he knocked at the door, then opened it to allow me inside. This room made my quarters in the castle look dismal and small, though they were not. Huge tapestries hung on the walls. A fire in the large fireplace was blazing away as it kept the day's chill at bay. In front of the fireplace, the King was sitting at a chess table. The chess board itself was quite dazzling. Its squares seemed to be made of White marble, that and black Ebony. Surrounded by a gold frame as its base. The pieces themselves of gold and silver, Each encrusted with gem stones.

As I approached, the King motioned with his hand for me to sit opposite him, which I did. He only grunted slightly as he pushed his Queen's Knight's Pawn, ahead two squares. I was instantly aware that either the King didn't know how to play a decent game of chess, or this was a challenge. As I handily won the game, I happen to look up to see Jonathan's face on my checkmate move. It seemed as if he was in pain.

Without thinking of protocol, and whom I was really sitting across from at the chess table, I said. "You opened your game weakly, your Majesty, and left your King open to my black Bishop, which was the death of your King. Perhaps, if you'll have me for a few days, I can help you to better your game openings?"

Now as I looked up, Jonathan was clearly shaken. I suddenly realized why. Here I was speaking to the King of Castile as if he were just another man. The King had seemed slightly upset at having lost, but after sitting back in his chair, and looking me straight in the eyes, for a few moments, he said. "I accept your offer. You will stay with me for a year to teach me how to play chess properly."

Again, my mind just jumped into my answer. "Your Majesty, I'm a traveling man. I cannot stay here for a year?"

He was having no part of my answer. "I will give you a talent of gold each seven days. To be collected upon your leaving my service.' In addition I will see to it that you are rewarded very well if my game improves significantly."

I must admit I didn't know how much a talent of gold was worth, as it was beyond my personal wealth, but I knew it was a goodly sum. Still, I was a bit reluctant. "Your Majesty . . ."

He interrupted me saying. "Also, I hear you are a man who plays for stakes?"

"I have played for stakes, your Majesty."

"Good. We will play for stakes as well."

I could sense my purse expanding even more. "What stakes might that be, your Majesty?" I was then greatly surprised at his next revelation.

"We will play one game a week for a life or a death."

"Life, or death, your Majesty?"

"Yes, if you win you can choose someone I have condemned to death, to live. If you lose, you must choose someone to die. Each time, Jonathan will see to your wishes, and will inform me two days after it is done"

He turned to look at his minister. "You understand you will carry out my instructions each time without fail, Jonathan."

"Jonathan bowed to his King and replied. "It shall be exactly as you wish, your Majesty,'

With that the King rose from his chair and left the room.

After the King left us, I asked. "Is he serious, Jonathan?"

"He is known as the Cruel King. Yes, he is very serious."

Before Jonathan and I parted company, and even thought I was shaken, I asked. "Jonathan, what is in the room under guard high in a tower room at the other side of the castle?"

"Why were you in that part of the castle?"

"Just wandering."

He looked at me stone faced before he answered. "It is the Queen's quarters."

"I didn't know there was a Queen in the castle."

"The King imprisoned her there some years ago. She made him angry and he has not forgiven her. She is, in essence, dead."

"Oh my. Well, how does she get by?"

"She has a lady in waiting, Miriam. Miriam sees to her every need."

"Why doesn't the King just let her go?"

"That would not be a punishment. Also, she has no direction or location with which to go."

"What did she do to anger him so?"

"She wanted to ease the tax burden that the people have to pay the crown."

"For that he imprisoned her?"

"Yes."

I began to play chess with his Majesty each day, it was three weeks later before he said. "Today we begin playing for stakes."

His game was improving steadily and now I was becoming concerned. As it turned out, I won the first game, and as a result, I had an old man I'd heard about in the catacombs of the prison released. He was near death, but I was to hear that he started recovering rapidly with the tender care of his family. However, the following week I lost a game for stakes, and again I turned to the prison. An old woman was barely alive having been beaten and pillaged by the guards. I asked Jonathan to see that she was put out of her misery.

The condition of having to choose a life, or a death, was extremely hard for me to comprehend let alone to accomplish. I knew I needed some kind of a solution to my dilemma. One night while lying in bed, I came up with a possible solution. The next day, during our usual counsel, I asked Jonathan. "Is it still true that you do not advise the King of my decisions about who dies and who lives, until two days following my decision has been fulfilled?"

"That is true."

"And he does not question my choice?"

"No, he does not question your choice and yes, he allows your choice each time as he agreed."

"And you fulfill my request without fail, or question?"

"To do otherwise, would be to fail my sworn duty to the King. I do as he instructs without question."

"Good. I have my next two choices in mind now."

"Do you wish to tell me now?"

"No. I will tell you when the time comes."

The following week the King and I, played a close game and the King's King ended up on the Queen's Rook square after he moved onto this square to escape my Kings Rook on my King's Knight three square, and he moved onto this square, to get out of check from my queen's Rook as it moved to the Queen's Rook seven.

He moved to this square expecting to become stalemated on his next move. However, again he overlooked my black Bishop residing on its original square of King's Bishop one. He was upset when I moved the Bishop to King's Knight two for checkmate. I'd told him before this Bishop would cost him dearly.

He chose to ignore its power. Only this time it would cost him in another manner as well.

After the game, when Jonathan came to me for my decision on who was to live, he was greatly surprised. After I told him of my choice, I asked, will King Peter, allow it to happen?"

"He won't like it, but yes, he will do so at your request."

The next evening, Miriam, the Queen's handmaiden, came to my door. She knocked, then peeking inside saying. "The Queen would like to speak with you."

"Very well. I'll be along in a few moments."

"No need. Her Majesty is here." With that she opened my door further, and the Queen came inside. Miriam came with her, but waited just inside the now closed door.

I stood immediately, but her Majesty said. "Please, do not fuss over me. Sit"

I sat back down on one of my chairs, and she sat on another one close by. She said. "I understand you are the chess player, Ricardus?"

"Yes, your Majesty."

"You are responsible for my freedom."

"I may have had a hand in the event, your Majesty."

"Thank you. If I can be of any help to you, please let me know."

"I will your Majesty, and there may be something in the near future."

"What might that be about, and how can I help?"

"You will know what is required at the time, your majesty."

"Very well. Good evening, Ricardus." With that she rose and left my room.

It pleased me to see her looking so fit after having been held captive for such a long time. The following week, when the game for stakes was to be played, I was ready. I rarely ever intentionally lose a chess game, unless of course it is for stakes. Even then it is to sweeten the pot, as it were. This time was no exception.

I must admit though, that the King's game ability was increasing, as well as his winning of games. He was listening to my advice and setting traps of his own as we played. This was one of those games that I saw the trap being put into place, but played as if I hadn't, and I seemed to have blundered into it. Within a short time the King said. Joyfully I might add. "Checkmate to you Ricardus. You lose another game."

I let the King enjoy his win, but later in my room, when Jonathan came to get my next decision on who was to die, I felt overjoyed at having lost.

"Whom have you chosen for death this time, Ricardus?" He too, was tiring of this game the King was playing with me.

When I told him, his eyes widened. I could see he was taken aback by my choice. Still, he smiled after a bit, and said. "It shall be done."

The next day there seemed to be a great deal of some kind of confusion going on within the castle walls. I wasn't aware of all of it, but not only was Jonathan busy, so was the King's physician, and his other counselors as well.

Late that evening Jonathan came to my room and said. "The Queen wishes for your attendance, in the King's throne room."

When I arrived, Jonathan, and several others of the King's court, as well as Miriam were present. However, the King was not. Seated in his place was the Queen herself.

She smiled at me as I entered the room and bade me forward. I stopped at her feet and she began telling me of what happened.

"It seems the King died in his sleep last night.

Apparently, a natural death. I, as the Queen, will now rule Castile. You, Ricardus will receive your talents of gold, as promised, plus an additional reward from me."

"I bowed deeply to her Majesty and said."Thank you, your Majesty."

She smiled broadly as she said. "An odd thing though. The Kings' physician found a black Bishop in the King's hand as he examined him for the cause of death."

Now, these many months later, and as I still travel, it is toward my homeland. I'm quite wealthy now and plan on settling down in one place. Perhaps to play an occasional game of chess.

CHESS IN THE MONASTERY

This has been a controversial chess piece for most of its history. In the beginning it was known as a 'Wise Man, or Counselor.' At one time, in Russia, a Queen could be the normal Queen, or she could be an Absolute Queen. An Absolute Queen could also move like a Knight. This chess piece was first called a 'Queen' in Italy, but it was somewhere in the 1490s that the first modern Queen was introduced and had the ability to move as she does today.

Until this method was accepted, the piece had been severely restricted in its moves. Queens only really began to exert some power in the game of chess as the Royal Queen's themselves, began to show more power in the world. This took place about the time that Empress Adelaide, and Empress Theophano of the Roman Empire had some influence on their husbands.

In Tibet, a Tiger reigns as the Queen on the chessboard. In the years up to 1200, the Queen was much weaker, she could only move one square diagonally. In the middle ages she became the strongest piece on the chessboard. This change in attitude was attributed to Queen Isabella of Spain. Mind you, this was the Queen who sponsored Christopher Columbus. The same Queen who started the churches inquisitions. The same Queen who was responsible for Holy wars. As late as the 1700s it was debated as to its original meaning. Even then some were upset to think a Pawn could change sex, and with the possibility of having two Queens on the board.

CHESS IN A FAR PLACE

In the late fifteenth, or early sixteenth century, there was a small Monastery to be found just this side of the spine of a starving mountain. The ridge was just high enough to prevent decent weather from infiltrating the arid land fanning out below the Monastery. The life of the sixty or so Monks who lived there was devoid of any known pleasure that the rest of humanity enjoyed. With the exception of one, that was a single ongoing chess game. When, or how this chess game came into being is still unknown. Of course the Monks had their ongoing daily prayers, the working in a sparse garden and harvesting what little they can to sustain life. The chess game is one thing that keeps the minds of the Monks off the deprivation of the simple things others enjoy.

The chess set that resides here, has black squares that appear to be black slate, and the others of a lighter stone. The chess pieces are carved out of Gray Granite. The oldest stone on earth, and one that is found in the earths mantel. One side speckled with black spots, the other side speckled with spots of pink. Like that of 'Rose Quartz."

Each new game is set up by the Abbott himself, then left for the Monks to play. It is not a game that two opponents sit down to play, instead it is a game left in the open for all to see as they transit the common passageway where it resides.

There is a coin of unknown age that has a chariot on one surface, and it is used to mark the even days of the month, and a large cross on the other side is used to mark the odd days of the month. The coin is moved from one side of the board to other side after each move is made, and is used to indicate which color is to make the next move. That, and on what day it is to be moved, odd, or even.

At any time, as a Monk passes by the game, if the move has not been made for that day, he may make the next move, he then turns the coin over and places it on the other side of the chessboard awaiting the next player. It goes on like this until the game is finished. No one knows who may make the final mistake that leads to the loss of a game, nor does anyone know who makes the final checkmate. Only the players themselves carry the shame, or pride of the final crucial moves.

A single game may take months to complete, or perhaps just days on a rare occasion. The only time the Monks may speak to one another, is during the morning meal. Most often the ongoing question is. "Have you seen the game today?"

THE MENTALITY OF CHESS

To those who do not play chess often, if at all, the mind of chess players may not be easily understood. To even comprehend the mental workings of a chess mind can seem daunting.

During the regular day's activities, a chess player can seem to be, perhaps, a rather normal person. But, in their minds they might be trying to solve a problem of some particular game in the past that went awry. His, or her, mind will be analyzing how the game could have ended had they played this piece, or that one.

This is not the case with every chess player. On average the normal Saturday wood pusher only sees a few moves ahead, if that. He, or she, often plays a game while just visiting with friends. Time is not of importance, nor is the fact of whether they win, or lose. To these millions of weekend chess enthusiasts, being a Pawn down would hold little meaning. To a Master player, it could spell doom for their game.

I was once honored to play chess with a Grand Master in Greenwich Village of New York. It took place as he waited for someone else who was scheduled to arrive and I just happened to be sitting nearby with a chess set on the table in front of me. He asked. "You up for a game?" Of course I replied, "Certainly."

We played a number of moves before the person he had been waiting for appeared, they shook hands and he explained to his friend that he would only be a few more moments. As he finished the game between the two of us. Then he became more serious. He said, to me. "Do you mind if I show you where you made your errors?"

"Of course I'd like to see any errors I might have made."

He smiled at my naivety and started by moving the pieces backwards in the order of play, then when he arrived back at the beginning of the game, he played each of our moves forward as the game evolved. It seemed as if nearly every move I'd made was an error, and he proved each of them to me.

I, in a sense, was like a child learning to play. To this day I cherish that game. It thrills me still to have listened to his explanations and watching as his hands moved gracefully from piece to piece. His mind seemed a thing of wonder, his courtesy to me, a thing of beauty. It does not bother me that I'll never be at that chess level, I simply do not have what it takes, for I am a simple wood pusher.

In reality, the chess mind is not unlike that of a great mathematician, or world renown musician. It never stops seeing numbers arrange themselves into theories beyond normal understanding. The musical notes on a sheet of paper that seem to play loudly in the mind of a musician, but not heard by others, and chess players who see chess pieces that seem to move without help from human hands.

These players think constantly of coming chess tournaments and openings they might use, tactics and strategies that might work against each challenger they encounter at the chessboard.

This kind of thinking is incomprehensible to the lessor accomplished chess players. To those who are not of this game depth, the truest beauty of a complicated game and the intricacies of the moves required to bring the game to its end, simply, for the most part, escape us.

However, you should not fret if you are not at, or anywhere near, this level of play, most chess players don't have but a slight understanding of this level of play, and will never miss the fact that it even exists.

A one time student of mine, as I was beginning his first lesson of the basic fundamentals of the game, asked. "How long will it take me to learn how to play chess?"

I explained. "You will learn how the pieces move withing twenty or thirty minutes. To learn how to play good chess will take your lifetime."

HOW THE PIECES VIEW THE GAME

THE QUEEN'S POINT OF VIEW

These dolts, have they no sense of direction? Do they not look beyond the end of their noses? What time they waste moving one Pawn after another, and all the while they leave my Knight and Bishop lying in their beds. They have moved the King's Knight and Bishop, but not far. I too have fears, such as the time the King's Knight moved twice and the second time he moved out onto the field of battle, and Lo, there just beyond him stood the dark evil Bishop. I just knew from his piercing black eyes that he was intending harm to me, and yes in a physical sense as well. Other times my own King has sent me on shopping trips, well yes, but he most often sends a Knight, or Bishop along as well. Sometimes even a Rook accompanies me.

I know they are to look after my well being, but sometimes they hang back at a distance and I have to wonder if they can really protect me from the others in my immediate area. Don't think I don't know what it's like to be taken, and yes, against my will, because I do know. It can be frightful, it can be painful, and it can be humiliating, well, perhaps ths isn't so always. I have to admit that sometimes I simply give of myself. Sometimes I pretend I've just entered a village where I should not be, and am taken, but not without cost.

Sometimes it is just fun. Some have referred to me as, "That Bitch." Others have referred to me as "Her Majesty." Often when the day is done, it is not me lying on the bottom of the bag, or box. It is. "His Majesty, the King." However, I am usually found with the Pawns lying on top of me, those playful devils.

THE KING'S POINT OF VIEW

Where are these people when I need them? And her Majesty, what is she doing, taking a nap again? The Bishops, mine and hers, they seem to be single minded, and yet they think in similar ways. Sometimes they coordinate their day's activities. But often this is not the case. The Knights, who knows where they are? Most likely galloping off across the countryside according to their own selfish needs. I know they have the ability to attack two, three, even four enemies at once, and yes they share their spoils with me, still, I' like them to keep in closer touch. Many times I'll send a Pawn out with a message to a Bishop, or a Knight, but do they return with an answer, no they do not. They just keep meandering further away from home as if there is no return.

It's tough being the King. Granted I am behind the castle walls, yet I know danger lurks from every direction. That's the reason I like to know where these people are. I have found that even my Queen wanders into places where she does little good. Trapped if you will, safe where she stands, but of little use to me at home should I need her. "Witch." I don't always favor taking another Queen, though there have been times when one of my foot soldiers has returned from the front lines of battle and given me a surprise. I always promote a good foot soldier. And, yes, I have had occasion to have taken a Queen different from my own, often of color, and enjoyed having her. Even if for only a short time.

THE BISHOP'S POINT OF VIEW

You ever wonder where the saying. "Pray tell . . . " came from? Well I hear it all of the time. If it's not the King saying it, it's the Queen. "Pray tell me why you're so narrow minded." Or, perhaps. "Pray tell, why you can't see what's to come. Are you wearing blinders, or something?" I mean what do they think I have, some kind of insight, or clandestine connections? The King's always saying."Go have a look will you?" So, where does he send me, well right out in the open for all to see.

Sometimes I'm allowed to hang back in a corner, and I can be very sneaky from back out of sight. Then I do pray. I ask for the opposing King's Knight's Pawn to move just one space. That's all, just one space. Then I can zip down the whole length of the chess diagonal to kill, okay to maim a Rook clear on the far side of the chess board. That is so much fun. Throughout history I've been blamed for many wrong doings. I mean what in God's name do they expect from me? I mean some people simply need to be burned at the stake. I do whatever I think is necessary to acquire things of value for my King. Okay, on occasion I just do things to shake up those in higher places.

THE KNIGHT'S POINT OF VIEW

This chain link garment I have to wear is a constant drag. You learn quickly not to rinse off the sweat under a waterfall on a hot day. If you do, it is only a matter of time and you find you cannot move about quite as fast as you once did. Shetland ponies hate children who want to practice becoming Knights. The weight of the chain mail is crushing to their spirit. As a Knight I'm on call twenty four hours a day, no matter what else I might be doing.

Sometimes this is not good. Why just a fortnight ago I was waiting in the smithy's shop whilst he was putting new shoes on my steed, and the King sent word he wanted me to just jump to it. The blacksmith offered me a loner, but a broom horse wasn't going to do it for me. I had to leave without my steed having gotten all four new shoes, the left rear one was well worn, even somewhat loose, but we'd have to make do. It's disgusting to hear your steed going. 'Clip, Clip, Clop, then the final Clip.' The result was that I found myself in the heat of battle with a steed who could not run well. Myself and the good Bishop were confronted by a Pawn that both of us could not escape from. It was to be the end for one of us. Of course you can guess what happened. My weakly shod steed was sacrificed to save the Bishop. Maybe it does pay to pray.

THE ROOK'S POINT OF VIEW

There is no doubt I am a straight shooter. There is no dilly dallying from my chosen path in life. I move straight into battle. Do I like it this way, well not always but I am a tower of strength and I can see over the heads of most of the King's enemies, which affords me some advantage? Sometimes I'm to be found close to the King himself, and I'm often found in the company of the Queen. She is pleasant to spend time with, and I am fond of her. To the extent that I might lay down my life for her? I've heard her mention to her ladies in waiting. "He's a square kind of guy. Never cuts corners, always on the straight and narrow." However, I find she uses me for her own needs, like keeping an enemy King locked in the last line of defense, especially if the two of us are out for a venture.

PAWN'S POINT OF VIEW THE

Rain or snow, they expect one of us to show up at the gate, or the drawbridge to stand guard duty. Most of the time I have a friend close at hand, or within easy reach. Don't misunderstand, as I am often called upon to travel long distances. It might seem a death march to some, but if I reach my goal my King rewards me with royal favors.

Do I get trampled on, of course? Do my feet get sore, or course? Do I like my job, not always? Sometimes I'm like a spy, I get to see what is going to take place before others behind me, and yes at times it is costly to my well being. When we wake, we listen as the orders come down the line. Each of us wondering when it will be us called out. More often than not we'll first hear, "Do I have any volunteers to do the Kings work?" And of course it is e2 that steps forward two steps, but that is why he is the King's favorite. I, on the other hand standing here on b2, am often used like a secret agent, or spy. I am able to sneak down the line to the end and obtain a favorable position on the deepest of enemy positions. I might add I am usually rewarded for having accomplished this maneuver. Still, after the first volunteer, we know it is only a matter of time before the rest of us get our marching orders.

INSECTS

I was in a small Greenwich Village chess club, and about to play chess with an older man, when he excused himself to refill his coffee cup. I'd seen the large coffee urn and the cream and sugar that was made available to those who wanted to use them. I'd also noticed that there were those who accidently spilled both of those items while they fixed their coffee.

After he refilled his cup. he came back to the chess table, sat down, took a sip of his coffee, and then made a Queen's Pawn opening. After a few more moves, and listening to other players comments about the games they were playing, he said to me.

"We have a few ants around here."

I replied, "That doesn't surprise me with all of the spilled cream and sugar over there by the coffee pot."

He looked at me rather surprised at what I'd said, then smiled as he said. "Oh, no. Not sugar ants, chess ants is what we have."

"Chess ants?"

"Yes." Then he went on to explain. "A chess ant is someone who studies all of the chess openings recorded in books."

I had never heard of this before, and said. "So, is that good or . . . .?"

He made another move that threatened my Queen, and said. " Oh. . . . well they know the openings, but most of the time they can't play a good game when it gets past the opening moves, or if the game deviates from the openings they've learned."

"So book learning isn't as good as you might think?"

"Oh, no, book learning is good, but you have to play chess to learn how to play chess."

THE CHESS CHEAT

I know you think people can't cheat at the game of chess, and now-a-days that is basically true. Not so in the days of old. A time when they were using sand glasses for timing the chess games during tournaments. As an example I happened to be in England and present during the opening games between a French champion, Jacques Bourdais and an Englishman, John Hillary.

It was the second game to be played in this match when I was present, and I saw what I thought an odd playing condition. It was the condition that aroused my curiosity. The thing that thing that was happening and that struck me as odd was caused by something I'd learned while at sea. Something I'd learned while I was aboard ship, and en-route here from New York. To be sure I watched the game for some time, each man in turn turning their glass on its side when it was their opponent's turn to play. The opponent's glass would then be turned up on its end so the sand would continue to flow.

This was a fairly new method of timing chess games and to control the timing of the event. Though it was a new method in chess, it wasn't without its problems. Each player kept a close eye on his opponent's glass as well as his own. Lest his opponent's glass, get turned back on its end, but turned up on the wrong end, the sand would flow again, but back from whence it had just come.

I watched the game in play for a spell longer, then I said to my host, Francis Bruin, the tournament director. "The Frenchman won the first game because the Englishman's time ran out, didn't he?"

He seemed astounded at my remark, he knew I had not been here for the previous game. "How could you know that?"

I smiled as I said. "The Frenchman cheats."

"Impossible. We watch every game closely. He is not cheating."

"How is it that the table placed where it is?"

"The Frenchman prefers the sunlight to come from the opposite side of the board. He says it gives him better light for his poor vision."

"And, wouldn't you agree that, that is highly irregular. Most players would avoid the shining sunlight while playing chess, especially coming toward them while seated at the board?"

"Yes, it is odd, but it is his preference."

"Also, the sand glasses, why are they in those positions?"

He looked at me questionably, then said. "The Frenchman has asked to have each player's sandglass on their right-hand side."

"He's cheating on the time."

"Impossible. We have someone watch each player's glass as it is turned, to be sure it is done correctly."

"Yes, but I still think he is cheating. You watch, if he wins this game because your English player runs out of time, I'll explain it to you."

I watched a short time longer, then took my leave to go for a refreshment across the street. Nearly two hours had passed from the beginning of the match game, and its ending. I was still in the Café across the street when the tournament director came to me. He sat down near me, ordered a coffee, then said. "The Englishman, John Hillary, ran out of time and in doing so, lost the game."

I smiled as I watched him squirm on his seat, finally he looked me right in the eye, saying. "How does he cheat?"

"He warms his opponent's glass."

"I beg your pardon. He does what?"

"Let me explain something, I learned from a ships Captain during my voyage to England. The Captain told me that the sandglass used for marking the time each of the watches, Port, or Starboard, were on duty, were under the helmsman's care. Each time the glass went empty, he would turn it over and ring the ship's bell to tell the hour. Then he also told me how a helmsman on the night watch had been caught cheating the sand glass."

"Is this something new?"

"Apparently, yes, and known only to a few."

"How does it work?"

"On board the ship, the helmsman would place the sandglass inside the compass binnacle housing. You see at night a small whale oil lantern is lighted so the helmsman can read the compass. When in reality, in this case, he was warming the glass with the heat from the candle. As the glass warms, it expands and allows the sand to flow faster. Thus, shortening the time, he had to stand watch on a cold night at sea."

I watched as Francis went over this in his mind, then he said. "What would you suggest I do about the condition at the tournament? I can't offend either player, but the condition must be addressed."

I'd already considered what could take place, so I told him my idea. "I'd close the drapes to stop the sunlight from warming the glass. Then place a lamp at the Frenchman's side and explain it will help his poor vision."

"If he complains?"

"Oh, I'm sure he will, but you can explain the sunlight is offensive to the others who have to observe the game, such as, yourself."

Several days later I stopped by the chess club and I had only been there a short time before the tournament director came to my side. "You see, we have provided a lamp as you suggested."

"Yes, and the drapes are pulled tightly together."

"Yes, and the Frenchman has been losing most of his games. Pity."

NAPOLEON BONAPARTE

As a young lieutenant Napoleon Bonaparte was, in reality, a poor chess player. He would make bold and unusual moves and most often played without a proper foundation as to the value of each move. He played as if his opponent could not possibly fathom what he himself was planning. Still, when he lost the game he often became rude, noisy, and argumentative. It often happened that he would upset the board and scatter the pieces in many directions.

In the end, when Napoleon was exiled to St. Helena he played chess daily. He made it a point to play a game of chess before he sat down to dinner each day. He played with a chess set sent to him by his French friends. It was a beautiful chess set. The board was made of Ivory and ebony with mother of pearl inlays. The pieces were of gold and silver. It became known years after his death that the young lieutenant, and officer with connections to his stance friends in France, and who was to deliver the set to him on the Island, died at sea and had carried a secret message known only to him, and was lost at his death.

The person who ultimately delivered the chess set to Napoleon was not aware of the secret compartment inside one, or some of the chess pieces. The compartments, were also unknown to Napoleon, but one of them held the plans for his escape from St. Helena.

After his death the chess set was given to his son, who quickly spent the families fortune and had to sell the chess set for more funds, of which he also spent. Over the years the chess set passed through many more hands. My understanding is that the chess set came up for auction with a well respected company in England. The newer owner had decided to clean the tarnished set, and in so doing found that the bottom of one of the pieces, I suspect the Queen, came loose. A small piece of parchment fell out, and after it was read by someone who understood French, it seems Napoleon's friends had offered him a way of escaping Saint Helena. He had only to send them a message as to his wishes.

Napoleon also had a thirst for ladies of the stage during the height of his military career. He would often take a fancy to one of them, and arrange for her to meet him in his bedroom. However, because of his duties as First Counsel of France, he often had to finish his daily work of that office. Because of this it sometimes happened that the lady waiting for him, waited for hours on end alone.

There was some furor when the lady, 'Mademoiselle Georges' spent an evening with him. It seems he fainted away after they had made love and she thought she'd killed him. She was very afraid she would be facing the Guillotine, but she avoided this by calling his servants, a doctor, and his wife, 'Josephine. Mademoiselle Georges, was of course very beautiful and still very naked at the time.

THOSE WHO WIN EACH GAME OF CHESS

You wouldn't think it mattered when you were born and your ability to play chess effectively. How the time you were born could have any affect on the outcome of your games of chess, and in what order you find yourself in the multitude of other chess enthusiasts. But, it does matter, and here's the result of those findings. There are those who will say this kind of information is nonsense. However, ancient chess history depicts otherwise.

Read the listings below to find yourself, and begin to watch those with whom you play chess, and apply what you learn.

This then is the pecking order of chess players. Whether it is in local clubs, or international tournaments. There are however, other strengths to consider that are beyond the scope of this book.

The beak down of each of the following is a basic list going from the strongest, to the weakest.

FIRST
Those who have birthdays between the last week of October and the third week of November. This is when the Sun is traveling through the constellation of Scorpio. Also, the strongest players are born between the hours of four to six P.M. Or eight to ten A.M. Plus or minus.

SECOND

Those who have birthdays between the last week of February and the third week of March. This is when the Sun is traveling through the constellation of Pisces. Also, the strongest players are born between the hours of eight to ten A.M. Or midnight to two A.M.

THIRD

Those who have birthdays between the last week of May and the third week of June This is when the Sun is traveling through the constellation of Gemini. Also, the strongest players are born between the hours of two to four A.M. Or six to eight P.M. Plus or minus.

Also sharing third place are those who have birthdays between the last week of September and the third week of October. This is when the Sun is traveling through the constellation of Libra. The strongest players are born between the hours of six to eight P.M. Or ten A.M. to noon. Plus or minus.

FORTH

Those who have birthdays between the last week of January and the third week of February. This is when the Sun is traveling through the constellation of Aquarius. Also, the strongest players are born between the hours of two to four A.M. Or ten A.M. to noon. Plus or minus.

FIFTH

Those who have birthdays between the last week of November and the third week of. December This is when the Sun is traveling through the constellation of Sagittarius Also the strongest players are born between the hours of two to four P.M. Or, six to eight A.M. Plus or minus.

SIXTH

Those who have birthdays between the last week of March and the third week of April. This is when the Sun is traveling through the constellation of Aries. Also, the strongest players are born between the hours of eight to ten P.M. Plus or minus.

SEVENTH

Those who have birthdays between the last week of December and the third week of January. This is when the Sun is traveling through the constellation of Capricorn. Also, the strongest players are born between the hours of six to eight A.M. Plus or minus.

Also, sharing seventh place are those who have birthdays between the last week of April and the third week of May. This is when the Sun is traveling through the constellation of Taurus. Also, the strongest players are born between the hours of four to six A.M. Or, Midnight to two A.M. Plus or minus.

EIGHTH

Those who have birthdays between the last week of August and the third week of September. This is when the Sun is traveling through the constellation of Virgo. Also, the strongest players are born between the hours of noon to two P.M. Or, eight to ten P.M. Plus or minus.

Also, sharing the position of eighth place are those who have birthdays between the last week of July and the third week of August. This is when the Sun is traveling through the constellation of Leo. Also, the strongest players are born between the hours of two to four P.M. Or, ten P.M. to midnight. Plus or minus.

NINTH

Those who have birthdays between the last week of June and the third week of July. This is when the Sun is traveling through the constellation of Cancer. Also, the strongest players are born between the hours of four to six P.M. Or, two to four P.M. Plus or minus.

WHICH PLAYER ARE YOU?

This classification system was drawn up by
T. E. Widdows and I believe he was with the Worchester
city chess Club at the time. I'll list them, and their
meanings, in the order he presented.

Drawist:
This player always wants, and asks for a drawn game,
and generally right after 1. e2-e4 , e7-e5. His smile, is
proportional to the material disadvantage in which he
finds himself, and when his offer is refused his pained
expression shows his anguish.

Rattler:
Having just taken a weekend seminar in Psychology he's
decided in making irregular openings. He begins with
d2-d4 and slams the Pawn down hard as he places it on
the board. With his hand removed he begins to glare at
his opponent, as if to say. "You lose." Often he is
frustrated when the opposing player decides to play an
additional ten moves just for show and tell.

Chair Manipulator:
You've no doubt seen this player in your own club. This
is the guy who tilts his chair back, rising up and resting
one foot on the seat while he looks at the board from
above. Or, he could simply twitch around on the seat
from side to side when it is the opponent's turn to play.

Pencil tosser:
After writing down his move, he tosses the pencil carelessly onto the table and watches it roll halfway across the surface as if he is considering making some kind of reckless move in the near future. Or, he may lay it down carefully, as if he has some subtle plan in effect.

New, non-smoker:
In days of old this was a rare player indeed, but in today's society it is common. Those who have just quit smoking are the ones who the kibitzers to watch closely. This one will wave smoke away, even nonexistent smoke. He'll cough loudly when anyone near him exhales as if he is about to pass out from the second hand smoke inhalation. He may even resort to covering his face with a handkerchief or any suitable material, even the hem of a shirt tail.

Body swayer:
This is a player who can actually become dangerous. Not only to himself, but to others around him as well. He'll begin by moving his body back and forth at alarming angles, but when he reaches the angle of no recovery, somewhere around thirty degrees, he could easily topple over. His falling can have a devastating effect as he can easily grab for something with which to stabilize himself and in so doing upset not only his own board, but perhaps others on the same table. When this happens, anger is sure to follow. In the end there could be an impromptu meeting of the club members which will be recommending his removal from the club roster.

Hand hoverer:

Most often this seems to be someone who cannot make up their mind as to which piece to move. They reach out for one piece, only to have their fingers stop just before touching the piece, then withdrawing as if to think it over a bit more. He'll tug at his ear lobe, tap his finger against his chin, smooth his hair back, even if he doesn't have any. However, you have to watch him closely. You see, he may just be making false advertisements, wanting you to think he is pondering that move soon, but makes another one beforehand.

Vocalizer:

This is the one who makes numerous noises as the game progresses. You will hear long "Ooohhhs" or "AAAahhs." And "Uuummph." Is another favorite, as is "Eeehh?" When he finds he is about to be checkmated, the noise level escalates dramatically. Surprise, or shock, even horror will register with those around close. Each noise will be determined by the game problem he finds himself facing.

The fake Annoyance, or gesticulating player:

Watch this player carefully, this can easily be one of the sneakiest players you find across the board from you. He'll make what seems to be a bad move by leaving a piece *'en prise,'* then make a gesture of annoyance as if he's made a mistake. Then when his opponent grabs the seemingly free piece and removes it from the board, he sees the trap that he has fallen into. Many traps, swindles, or pitfalls have taken place by this kind of player.

Hair, arranger:

This one has caused untold chess arguments. He is constantly running his fingers through his hair, as if combing it with each pass. The problem occurs when this is someone who uses hair oil. You see, when it is his turn he picks up a piece and makes a move. However after he has touched a piece, usually more than once, it becomes, shall we say . . . slippery. As he picks up a Pawn, it slips from his finger tips, drops onto the board, and suddenly as he places it back onto the board, it is now a passed Pawn that seems to have advanced further than it was thought to have been. Perhaps even Queening soon.

Glasses cleaner:

Another player to be watched closely. He'll pull his glasses from his face, look at them in disgust and mutter something like. "No wonder my game has been suffering." Out of his pocket will come a large handkerchief with which to clean them, and in so doing it sweeps across his side of the board knocking pieces all over the place. By the time they are replaced, he may have castled on the Queen side rather than the heavily attacked King side.

Table tapper:

Finger nails are the key ingredient here. The harder they are, the more they can be hammered on the table top. You may even notice callouses on the end of his fingers.

Whistler:
The worst part of this person noise is that they don't whistle in tune. Or, perhaps it is a happy tune, such as "Happy birthday to you." Over and over.

Leg and foot mover:
You may not see the ongoing movement, but you know it's taking place. You know because their body is moving a bit with each swing of the leg, and you see their body undulate in time with the moving knees.

Nose tweaker:
He may just be reaching up often to grip his nose, move it from side to side, as if he has a nose hair tickling him, and he could have. Or he may sniffle rather than just blow his nose, this is a ploy which he may use later when he needs to rearrange his chess pieces with a large handkerchief.

Shoulders and elbows:
This can be an interesting person to watch. As his shoulders begin to shift back and forth, watch to see if his elbows start moving as well. You may be seeing someone who is contemplating taking flight. But, if he starts to crow, you'll know he's just a farm boy at heart.

BIRTH OF TOURNAMENTS

It was an idea that had been entertained for years, but no one knew quite how to bring it about. Then, on May 26th of 1851, a committee of 'Tournament Management,' was formed and led by Howard Staunton.

The first meeting was used to set up the rules to be used, and of which would never even be considered in the years to come. It was decided that there would be no time limit placed on the duration of the games, the opponents would simply play until the games were won or lost. The tournament was to be a 'Knockout,' tournament.

This is in reality a 'One Life,' tournament, if you lost a game, you were out of the tournament. If you won your game, you moved onto the next round. The 'Round Robin' and 'Ladder,' tournaments were still to come in the future.

The first tournament was played in the 1862 London International Tournament. Even the hourglass was a thing yet to take place in the future of chess. It was decided the winner of a round would have to win two games out of three, and that winner would face the other winners in the next round of play.

The equivalent of $25.00 was to be the entry fee and the winner of the tournament would be awarded one third of the money gathered from entry fees. From there it was divided downward so that even the player who placed sixth would be given some prize money.

To find out who was going to play against each other, they used a pairing system that was decided by drawing tickets. There were an equal number of white and yellow tickets to be drawn and each color was numbered in a numerical sequence. With the exception that whomever drew a white ticket, had the choice of color they wanted to play and they also had the first move.

The result was that a person who drew a white ticket could choose to play the black chess pieces, but still have the first move. With this in mind, whomever drew the number six white ticket would play whomever drew the number six yellow ticket. So it was with all the numbers drawn.

CHESS IN THE BEGINNING

The beginning of chess is, and will remain an area of controversy. Unless it started as Knuckle Bones. Many believe it came to be somewhere in the mid fifth century. However, the Polish Orientalist F. Machalski indicated it there was something to be found in Persian Literature of the Sassanid period of A.D. 242-650

The chess pieces have run amok for years on end, and so have the chessboards. Though we normally use a standard chessboard of 64 squares, unless you are involved in a game of partnership chess, which is played on a board of 160 squares.

Arabic chess
The Queens were very limited, and they could only move one square diagonally. A Bishop's limit was a three square move diagonally, but it could jump over another piece in its path. Somewhere along this same time period the Rook could only move two squares.

Spanish chess
About 1560, in Spain, a King which had not moved and not in check, could jump two squares in any direction as long as it was not into, out of, or across check. The castling condition we now use seems to have come from France about this same time period. The rule was if the space between the King as his Rook, was vacant, the King could move two spaces and the Rook would come around to the King's vacated square.

Italian chess
Castling went through a good many options over time, such as in 19th century Italy, they had a "Free Castling" method. In which the King could move to any square beyond the Rook, and the Rook could move to any square up to, and including the King's square.

Icelandic chess
Here the King was allowed to make one move during the game similar to that of a Knight.

India Chess
In ancient India chess was a military game used to teach officers and their leaders the art of war. In many countries the chess pieces became inanimate. Not so in India, here though they may have changed in power and shape, they always remained human.

Sumatra chess
A pawn is not promoted to any other piece when it reaches the eighth rank on a chessboard, it simply is moved back to its original square and starts its journey all over again.

Chinese chess
Hsiang-chi came from Chatrang. It is played on a rectangular board of nine by ten points. The River, in the center of the board separates the two armies. The pieces

move along the lines and stand at the intersections of those lines. They are usually disks that are marked on top as to their value in the game. They have generals, Chancellors, counselors, who are like Bishops. There are also Chariots, like our Rooks, and horses like our Knights, but they cannot leap over other pieces. Pawns move one point forward until they cross the River, then they can move sideways, as well. There is also a chess piece that moves like our Rooks but is called, Cannons.

Japanese chess

The General's game, or Shogi, is played on a board of nine by nine squares, but is devoid of color. The chess pieces are all of the same shape and color, but have markings on the top to indicate their value in the game. The direction they travel is denoted by a corner, which is always pointed at an opponent. Each player has twenty pieces of eight different kinds. They have three kinds of Generals, and precious stones were used for the most valuable of generals. This is followed in order of rank by the gold general, who is followed by the silver general. They also use Knights, Bishops, Rooks and Pawns, but they are not called by those names.

Arithmetical chess

This was a very complicated chess game, and it seems it was a game that only resembled chess. It took a mathematical mind to even play the game because of its complicated rules. The chessboard was divided into 128 black and white squares. Eight squares by sixteen squares, and each player had twenty-four chess pieces. There were three kinds of chess pieces, round, square, and triangular, all moving in different directions.

Alcoholic Chess
This game is played on a chessboard with larger squares, but instead of the normal chess pieces you will find a variation of drinks depending on the player's decisions. It may be bottles of beer for the pawns, perhaps a good bottle of wine for the Bishops, a bottle of Brandy for the Rooks, maybe Vodka for the Knights, and you could use a Magnum of Champagne for the Queen, and fifth of whiskey for the King. The choices are up to the drinking habits of the players. One rule that brings the game to a quick end, is that when a piece is captured it must be drunk in its entirety before the next move can be made. Lasker is said to have sacrificed his Queen and his opponent had to drink a quarter liter of Cognac before continuing the game. Of course he was so incapacitated he could not continue and so he lost the game by default.

Living Chess
Using people as chess pieces on a large chessboard, indoors, or out, has been taking place for centuries. It is said that Charles Martel of the seventh, or eighth century was given credit for having introduced living chess in Europe. The earliest written account of living chess was to be found in records written by an Italian Dominican Friar, Francisco Colomna about the year of 1467. In 1554 the Italian town of Marostica witnessed a chess

duel for the hand in marriage of the governors' daughter. In 1562, and in the court of Dame Quintessence, a strong believer in chess, A live chess game took place that was apparently quite extravagant. Not only in players, but in the pomp and circumstance that went with it for royalty. There is a copper engraving depicting a live chess game in a French court in 1640.

When Alekhine spent time in China, in 1933, he watched a live chess game take place in a city square. I'm to understand that Strobeck Germany also keeps a living chess tradition alive. Since motion pictures came into being, several films using 'live chess,' have also been made.

CHESS WITH THE BATAKS.

In visiting the Bataks which is a tribe located high in the mountains of Sumatra. Early this morning I found an excitement pulsing though the village and soon I was given the reason why. It seems that there is a chess game to be played this very night, and it is to be one of considerable expense to its players.

I knew of the large chessboard to be found in the community center. It is constructed with beautiful and brilliant colors, the squares are large and will accommodate live players. I knew of live chess from my visits to parts of Europe, but it seems this may have been the original home of this kind of game. As I drank an alcoholic beverage with the village headman and, had I known beforehand how it was made, I might have only sipped a small amount of it to begin with. I was doing this so as not to seem rude in refusing the headman's invitation. As I sat near him, he went on to explain how this game was to be played. It seems that only the males of the village are allowed to play, and stakes are always offered as a prize to the winner. He also told me that, in essence, jeering is allowed. It has been my experience that kibitzers in any form are not always welcomed openly, so I learned early on to keep my mouth shut. Well most of the time.

When nightfall came and the community center was fully lit by flaming torches, the chosen players were cast in Erie shadows around the room. I was not seated next to the village headman now, as his counselors were close at hand.

I was across the room and seated next to one of the games judges. I was not aware of the total stakes involved, but I did know one of the men had to put up one of his favored wives to meet the challenger's wager on the outcome of the game. She would not be pleased to learn of this, and even more displeased if he lost the game.

As it turned out it was not to be a fast game. I myself would have made a couple of sacrifices to open up an area of attack against one of the Kings, but perhaps that is why I lose a good many games as well. They play the game as much of the world does, but seem reluctant to part with so much as a Pawn. It is often hard to observe the movement of the pieces on this large of a board, and especially while sitting down with your legs tucked under you. I'm not sure I could get up in any kind of hurry, as my knees and legs rebel at this kind of treatment. Still I could see that a great deal of maneuvering was taking place and moves being made that I had not foreseen being put into play. Moves that I myself would have missed the importance of, and of course lost the wife if I had placed her on the list as part of my wager.

The game lasted for nearly two hours before any pieces were being captured and threatening moves were made. Men in the room were cheering and a few moaning as their own personal wagers on the outcome of the game were being won or lost. To add to the confusion, the men, and boys, being used as the chess pieces were being moved about the chessboard, were drinking the same beverage I had been consuming with the village headman earlier. This was resulting in some stumbling about the board and causing arguments among the two men playing the game. Each in turn claiming, the piece had been on this or that square prior to the bumbled stumble. These were settled by the judge by whom I sat. How he could be sure of his decision I could not tell, but his decision stood and that was all there was no questioning his authority.

When the end of the game came, it surprised all of us. A trap had been set and one that was highly effective. It kind of reminded me of the Legal's mate, but it wasn't. It was tricky and depended on the opponent's greed. When he took the seemingly free counselor, used like our Queen, he lost the game. His anger surfaced rapidly at his own ignorance and harsh words were spoken between the two opponents. Quicky the village headman stood, and in the old language of the tribe he spoke softly, but his words had an impact. The game stood as it was, and the outcome noted. The wages were to be paid and that was the end of the discussion.

After the room quieted, I asked the judge, who was still seated next to me, what had finally taken place, he said. "The headman threatened to shut down the chess games for a year if they quarreled any further."

I was also to learn the man who won the game was to keep his wife, which had angered his opponent because he had wanted this woman as his own. In time I also learned that few Europeans ever win a chess game against these men.

THE CHESS CODE

This story comes from the sixteenth century. Anastasio was, as a child, saved from the remnants of a shipwreck by an Italian doctor with a mysterious background. The doctor, an alchemist, taught the boy mathematics, and upon his death he bequeathed to the young man, one hundred sequins, and a chess set. (An Italian sequin was a gold coin weighing 3.5 grams of pure gold.) With this new found wealth he decided to travel the land, and like any young man with money, he spent his wealth freely. That is, until one day as he prepared to pay his bill at an expensive hotel, he found he didn't have sufficient funds.

He knew he would have to sell something to raise the money he needed and he began to look through his belonging for something of value. He fingered his mathematical instruments, and knew he would need them for his teaching position when he arrived at Palermo, his final destination. He had already given away his old clothing, and couldn't sell his new ones. His decision came when he looked at the chess set he'd inherited from the good doctor.

Chess sets were of great value and not many could afford to purchase a good set. As he was taking one last look at the chessmen, he took them out of their case to fondly look them over.

Doing so he happened across a folded piece of paper wrapped around the inner edges of the case that he had not noticed before.

When he extracted the folded piece of paper, he began to examine it closely. Close scrutiny revealed several drawing of over a dozen chessboards marked with different chess piece combinations. Also some handwriting in the doctors hand that took him some time to decipher. In essence it read, "An infallible way too win every game of chess." Thinking back, he recalled having never won a game of chess against the good doctor.

His study of the diagrams took several hours, but in the end he remembered he had to go downstairs to pay his debt. With a heavy breath he found his purse, tucked the chess set under his arm and went downstairs. As he arrived in the Parlor he came across several friends, too embarrassed to admit his financial condition, he exclaimed. "My, my. I've forgotten my money. I meant to bring one more sequin, but look at this lovely chess set. Would anybody like to play a game?"

"Chess?" Replied Pescatini, the keeper of the hotel. "Indeed: we can play for the sequin you owe."

Someone remarked when overhearing the stake, said. "Then he'll have to go up for two sequins, as Signor Pascatini is an excellent chess player." The first game was started and Anastasio was down several pawns, all to the doctor's perceptions, but then he checkmated the hotel keeper and won the game.

Pascatini slapped at his forehead exclaiming. "AAAHHhhh, no it cannot be." Those who had gathered around the table laughed freely. Then he continued. "How was it I got caught so easily, but we'll play again and I will double the stakes."

This time Anastasio played more slowly, making his moves much more carefully, as a result the game took longer to get through. Both men were alert as they took one piece after another, until finally . . . "I've checkmated you again Signor Pascatini."

Pascatini was frustrated as he said. "Am I so stupid?" He thought for only moments before he said. "I'll raise the stakes six times as much."

Because Anastasio was having much more confidence in the doctor's formula, he said. "So be it."

This game was played with great tension all around, sweat pouring from the brows of both men. The game teetered back and forth as if a balancing act, but in the end, Anastasio, by a brilliant triple sacrifice, was able to deal a death blow to his opponent. A fork caught both the King and Queen under attack and within a few moves Pascatini was again checkmated.

Outraged, Pascatini said. "I don't believe this. Do you mind if I again raise the stakes?"

"To what extent?" Asked Anastasio.

"For twenty four sequins . . . Do you agree, signor."

"Why not indeed?" replied Anastasio.

This game took longer than any of those played previously and Anastasio was very confident in his interpretation of the doctor's theory. The result was the same, a checkmate to his opponent's King. After the game was completed, the hotel keeper began to walk up and down the room as others played against Anastasio. Each of them also losing a sequin, or two, to him. Later, up in his room, Anastasio counted his winnings. He had won 90 sequins for his day's efforts.

The next morning, Pascarini made an offer to, Anastasio. "Why don't you remain a guest of the hotel? I'll introduce you to other chess players as a foreigner traveling through the land who plays chess. We can arrange a stake and I'll get half and you the other half."

"Why would you get half when I do all of the work playing the game?"

"Signor, I'll be providing your quarters, the salon where you play, introductions, collecting the stakes, Perhaps a few meals. . . ."

"I see, and I understand, and I agree."

In the end, Anastasio spent so much time at the hotel playing chess, gaining a reputation and wealth, that by the time he arrived in Palermo his teaching position was gone to another, and the father of the woman he had wanted to wed, had also found another suitor and she was betrothed.

THE LATCH KEY KID

Powder Mill started as a coal town, well at least that was what had been expected in the beginning. The two brothers who found the coal vein had been so excited at the width of the vein on the surface that they bought a few cases of dynamite, and a front loader. By the time they had used the first case of dynamite they had a big empty hole in the side of a hill and the coal mine was empty. They had simply hit a surface pocket of coal, nothing more. Next came logging, but that too, had run out. Now, Powder Mill is a sleepy little bedroom town over the hill from a small city where most of its inhabitants commute to and from work each day. In the beginning in the town of Powder Mill, there had been one small gas station, one small market, and the Powder Mill Café.

Then chess was introduced into town, this came about because of Bobby Fischer's raising such a ruckus all over the world in his sudden rise to chess fame. Just as quickly there was a chess set on every dining table, or maybe the coffee tables in each living room, and in almost every home in Powder Mill as well.

Trouble was, most of the folks who had these chess sets didn't know how to play chess. The few that didn't have a chess set displayed began to think of themselves as imbeciles, and they began to ask questions. Like. "How do you play this game?" Or make comments such as. "I didn't know you knew how to play chess?"

This of course caused a ripple affect, and within a short time you couldn't find a book on chess anywhere around the area, not even in the city over the hill. The few that could play chess also found out they couldn't play very well, and because of their friends wanting to learn how to play the game from them, they too had to improve their game.

Phil, the owner of the local café suddenly realized how he might save his floundering café. Business had dropped off so much that he'd had to lay off his help and run the place by himself. Now, however, an opportunity had arisen and he'd set to work. He removed most of the restaurant's kitchen area, then gutted the rest of the interior of his café. Within a month he had completely rebuilt the insides of the place, and he had purchased many good, and very comfortable overstuffed chairs. Along with some nice tables to put chess sets on between the chairs, and some very good wooden chess sets. The garish lighting was replaced with softer lighting, mostly lamps, and the floor had been carpeted. The sign out front now read. "Powder Mill Chess Club." It hadn't taken long for word to get around and the chess players from town were inside each day to play chess with anyone who was open to a game. Generally what took place was that upon entering the club, they would meet with Phil who sat at a short counter close to the door. From him they would rent a chess set, and sit at whatever table was open, or their favorite table if it was available. Or, upon entering they might look around to see if someone else was waiting for an opponent, which was all to common.

Phil offered sandwiches, canned soda's, and snacks to players when they wanted them, and this kept him in enough funds to live a decent life style.

One afternoon, when the club was still empty, Phil watched the local school bus let its wards off on the corner across from his club, and he watched the kids meander off in various directions toward their homes. All except for one young boy. He'd seen this boy before and knew he lived close by, but today as he watched the boy, he seemed to be studying the chess club. Shortly he walked over to the café door and came inside.

He looked around, turned to Phil, and said. "Is it okay for me to come in here?"

"Not a problem for me young son, but, you should know this is a chess club."

"Yes, sir. That's why I'd like to come in."

Now Phil became curious. "You play chess?"

"Some."

"I see. Your momma gonna be worried when you're late getting home?"

"She isn't home yet. She works in the city over the hill."

"How old are you?"

"Ten, sir."

"Tell you what, why don't you come around here and use my phone to call her and tell her where you are."

"Okay." He put his books down on a chess table, then picked up the phone and Phil watched him punch in the numbers.

"Hi, Mom. It's me." Phil watched him as he spoke to his mother.

"I'm fine, Mom. I'm at the chess club. Can I stay here for awhile?" Then the boy looked up at Phil, and said. "She wants to talk to you."

Phil took the phone from him, raised it to his ear, and said. "Yes'm."

"I'm Anna. Teddies mother. He loves to play chess and has asked me several times if he could go to your club. Is it okay if he stays there for a time?"

"Anna, I'm Phil and I don't think Teddy will be a problem. If he gets underfoot, I'll send him home. If not, you can pick him up here on your way home."

"Phil, thank you so much."

"You betcha."

Phil knew then that he had a latch Key child standing next to him. One that spent several hours alone each day, and one that he himself would welcome here each day..

"Teddy, why don't you put your stuff around here on the shelf. Then go get a soda out of the refrigerator in the kitchen, and there are some bags of snacks and stuff on the table there, you can help yourself to them too. Then come back here and get yourself a chess set. You can set it up at any table you like and we'll see if anyone wants to play a game with you."

Teddy had set up the chessboard at table number three, the one in the southwest corner of the room. A favorite of most of the club's members because it had the best view. Less than an hour later, the Judge came in. I should let you should know he is a retired judge but the people in town still refer to him by the title of, "The Judge."

The Judge stopped at the counter by Phil, looked down the room toward the boy, then said. "We have a new member, do we?"

"Don't know Judge. Claims he knows how to play?"

"Bring me a cup of coffee, will you? I'll go see if he wants to play chess with an old man."

"Yes'sir. Be right there."

Within an hour there were several more players in the club, but they weren't playing chess, they were all crowded around the table where the Judge was playing chess with a neighborhood youngster.

They were all drinking coffee, or tea. One or two had sodas, and a good share of them were munching some kind of snack. Phil had done more business in this last hour, or so, than he did in any afternoon as a rule. He was down delivering a refill for cups of coffee because no one was coming to him for the refills. Mostly he was just curious.

At the outskirts of the group he asked one of the regular players. "The Judge giving the boy lessons, is he?"

He turned to Phil. "The Judge hasn't won a game yet."

"You're foolin with me?"

"Nope Seems to me like this kid is one a them prodigy types."

It was about five thirty when a young woman came in the door. She came directly to Phil, held out her hand and said. "I'm Anna, Theodore's mother."

Phil took her hand, smiled at the boy's name, then said. "Anna, I assume your boy is a latch key child, and I have no problem with that. But tell me. Does he get an allowance?"

142

"Yes, but it is small. I'm a single mother and it's expensive to raise a child these days let alone keep a household going."

"Anna, this is just between you and me, but I'll pay you a weekly fee that you could share with Teddy, if you'll let him come over here to play chess a few days a week. Starting after school, or whenever it's possible."

She thought about this for a few moments. She looked around at the surroundings, and at the men, and the one woman watching her son play chess.

"We can try that if you like. But you must know Teddy will want to come here every day. He loves this game."

Word had spread rapidly and every afternoon Phil would have to answer the same question over and over every time the phone rang. "Is Teddy playing today?"

"Yes, he is."

"I'll be right there."

It wasn't long before Phil had a teenage girl offer to work for tips to help him manage the coffee and food part of the business. Turns out she was making more in tips than he could have paid her in wages.

He'd started to refurbish the place. Buying new and more comfortable chairs, better chess sets, and having fresh pastries delivered daily for the clubs members. The place had become so crowded that every table was filled to capacity so the players could hone their skills. Each of them waiting a turn to play chess with Teddy. Phil maintained a list of players waiting to play chess with the boy, and the list was posted behind the counter. It was not a short list.

FIRST TO MOVE

When chess began to take its place in Persia around 600
to 650 AD, one of the Persian Shahs, 'Chosroes.' Loved
the game and played it on a regular basis. The Shah,
however, had his own personal oddities and one was the
fact that he also enjoyed wearing robes of a fine white
linen.

Being the Shah, or King of his land, he made it a rule
that he was the only one to wear robes of white, everyone
else were instructed to wear darker colors. Also as he
was the Shah, he always assumed it was his right to
make the first move in any chess game he played.

An important Raja, in his native land of India, had sent
an envoy bearing gifts to the Persian Shah, Chosroes. Of
which his spokesman, was warned before hand not to
make any mistakes which would anger the great Shah.
On his arrival in Persia the Shah's court minister, who
controlled the audiences with the Shah, made the
decision to let the envoy rest a few days before
presenting their gifts to the Shah.

Niogi, the head spokesman, knew before they arrived
that the Great Shah was someone who enjoyed the game
of Chess, of which he too, was a masterful player. One of
the gifts he'd been instructed to deliver was of a very
Ornate chess set. It pieces were of gold and silver, the
chess board was of Ivory and Ebony with a gold base.

While he awaited the audience with the Shah, he explored the marketplace looking for gifts to take home to his own family and his master the Raja. He also stopped to order clothing to wear while being presented to the Shah.

As he spoke with the best tailor in the city, he mentioned that he was here to have an audience with the Shah, and that he was going to ask him to play a few games of chess. The tailor began to show him different colors of his finest Muslim, but Niogi asked, "Do you not have some white Muslim?"

"I do, Master, but I cannot sell any of it to you. All white Muslim is held only for the Shah's use. You may have any other color, but not white."

After leaving the tailors shop, Niogi watched all in his surroundings. He did not see anyone else dressed in white. The next afternoon his group was summoned to the Shah's palace, and upon arriving, he spoke with the Shah's minister, he said. "I understand the Shah plays chess?"

The minister looked at him quickly. "Yes, he does. Do you know the game?"

"I am quite skilled in the game." He knew this was not quite so, but he wanted to play chess with the greatest Shah of all time.

The minister replied. "I shall speak of it to the Shah."

The envoy from India was presented to the Shah, the gifts given, and then just before their audience was dismissed, the minister went to the Shah's side, knelt down close and whispered in his ear. The Shah nodded, looked out at the envoy, smiled, and spoke to his minister. As the envoy was leaving the great hall the minister came to, Niogi, and said. "You are expected to join the Shah this evening. I believe you should expect to spend a great many hours playing chess."

"I shall be ready."

"One more thing you should know, White moves first."

As he freshened himself in his quarters in preparation for the upcoming games of chess, it finally dawned on him. As the great Shah, Chosroes, is the only one allowed to wear white Muslim in this kingdom and that he is the only one who is allowed to move his chess piece first.

LEONARDO GIOVANNI

Leonardo was born in Cutri in Calabria, and as a young man his family sent him to Rome to study law, a profession that they approved of and wished for their son. However when he arrived and found his quarters to his liking, he began to look about for something to take up his time when his studies allowed. What he found was a group of men deep in thought, and they were playing chess. He soon found chess much more attractive than his studies of law. As he mastered the game, he also found his ability at the chessboard had gained him a reputation as someone to play against. After a short time he became very well known, he was beating all of the players in the surrounding area. His youthful appearance soon gained him the nickname, "The boy."

In 1560, the Spanish Priest, Ruy Lopez, visited Rome where he heard about 'The Boy' and a game was arranged. However the one game that had been arranged ended up with the two men playing chess for two days. Leonardo was beaten so badly that after the priest left the city, he traveled to Naples and for two years he immersed himself into hours at a time to study the game that he thought he had known so well.

While in Naples, word reached him of news that his brother had been captured by pirates, and they were demanding a ransom of 200 Crowns for his safe return. Leonardo did not have that kind of wealth, but he heard the pirate captain played chess.

Daring to take the chance he challenged the captain to play chess. The captain, himself an accomplished player, accepted the challenge.

The wager was for the release of the brother of Ruy Lopez, that, and he felt he could also win a few gold coins as well. The games started early and when they had finally gotten to the point that the captain realized he was no match for his adversary, he relinquished his prisoner, and by this time he had also lost a large sum of money besides.

Leonardo, bolstered by his success on the pirate captain returned to Rome and upon finding Ruy Lopez within the city, he challenged him to a match. The match was to take place in the King's court, and when Leonardo won the game, King Phillip rewarded him with 1,000 crowns. He also, upon Leonardo's request, granted Leonardo's native town exemption from taxes for 20 years.

However, once again in Naples his popularity caused jealousy among his rivals. No one could beat him in chess and ill feelings were caused. In the end someone in his circle of acquaintances poisoned him and he died at the age of 45.

DEATH OF A TSAR

I myself had been in need of a physician and had been fortunate enough to have found that I could have access to the Tsar's physician himself. This only happened because I was in the royal palace when I became ill, well actually I only had a cold, but the condition did not escape the Tsar's doctor.

He was about to treat me with some kind of goopy salve when the Tsar's physician was called to his Majesties bedside. I was not aware of it at the moment but the Tsar himself, in bad health.

The doctor began to gather his medical kit and not knowing what else to do, I followed him as he rushed from the room. Quickly and quietly we rushed down dark corridors until we came to a large ornately carved doors where guards stood on each side. As I seemed to be with the doctor, they did not question my right to enter the Tsar's bed chamber. Inside I stood back out of the way as the doctor advanced to the bedside and began to feel the Tsar's neck and wrist for his pulse. It seems he was alive, but barely.

The Tsar was in a state of mind that was one of anger, he was going to die, but he was denying and defying its coming. As he lay in his bed he called out to a man.

"Rodovone, bring me my chess set." This would be Rodovone Boerken, one of the Tsar's favored friends.

The chess set was brought forth, given to the Tsar, and he began to set up the board as for normal play. Other of the Tsar's favorite personages were in the room at the time, and each watched as the pieces were being set in place. The Tsar was mumbling and fumbling as he tried to place the Kings on their squares. He couldn't get them to stand up correctly. It may have been the angle of the chessboard as this was taking place while he was bedridden and the chess set was at his side on top of the bed covers.

Boris Fedorowich started forward to help the Tsar get the Kings in place, when suddenly the Tsar, rose up sharply, then fell backward, and to lie still. The physician rushed to the Tsar's side, and again checked for his pulse. After a few seconds he raised his face to the others nearby and swung his head from side to side indicating it was too late. The Tsar was pronounced dead. He had met his final checkmate.

WHO REALLY LOST THE GAME

King Canute started his life as the Prince of Denmark, Norway. He was a man of vision, and sought for himself positions of great power. Through the years of Viking activity his presence as a military giant, and a man who was quick to anger if things didn't go his way, led him to crown himself King of Norway, his homeland. It was only a few years later that he became the King of England as well.

On a more personal level one of the things he loved most was the game of chess, and he played it for hours on end. His servants were well aware of the long hours needed to attend to the King and his chess guests. All night chess games were commonly played in his private chambers, which required someone to be in attendance for any of the King's many, and ongoing needs.

In chess circles it is common for a player to ask, of be offered the chance to take a chess move back, perhaps one that would ruin his, or her chance of winning the game. Most often permission is given by the opposing player to do so. Both players then have a mental understanding that it is, in reality, an entirely different game that is now being played.

However, in 1027 King Canute, now of the British Isles, was playing chess with a Danish Earl on St. Michaels Eve. The night was cold, damp and one that made the King somewhat miserable and irritable. He, and the Earl, had played several games of chess, each of which had been a close battle between the two minds. It would not have been the last game of the night, but it was the one that sealed the Earls fate. It was shortly after the first few opening moves that the King made a horrendous error in play. An error that would no doubt quickly cost him the game and in a very short time. The error was one that was easily seen, and easily understood to have been one made without thinking clearly, and one of embarrassment.

The King looked over at the Danish Earl, and said. "I've made the wrong move. I'll put it back and move the piece I should have moved."

Before the King could return the offending piece back to its original square, the Earl said. "No. You made the move, let it stand."

The King was infuriated at the Earl's insistence of his leaving the costly move as it was, and they both knew the game was soon to be a win for the Earl.

Without further thought the King called his guards and had the Danish Earl put to death.

IS THIS YOU?

You like to play chess, you really do, but you're not an avid player. You like to play but not in tournaments, or in really competitive games. You're simply not that aggressive and this is the reason you'll always remain just a "Wood Pusher." You've seen what happens to this kind of competitive chess player, as an example you know they keep notes on their calendars of the next tournament. When it will take place, and where. They try to dismiss it from their minds until then, but you know they can't. And in the weeks and days ahead they begin to fuss about making the arrangements for their lodging near where the tournament is to be held.

You're aware they try to find any information they can on those listed that they may play chess with, they do this so that they can study the favored openings of those players. So what do they do in-between these events, they practice as much as they can. You have seen some of this type of chess player and know they also play in any club ladder games, or round robin games that their club might put on.

Wood pushers, such as yourself, simply enjoy the game. You play chess this way so you have no pressure too win. You do this because you simply don't care if you win or lose. You, are really like most chess players, you like the comradery of other players like yourself. You like the chit chat that takes place.

You enjoy the lies each person tells, and all of those present knowing full wells they are lies. You may enjoy watching tournaments in play, and you become aware of missed moves. Move so obviously that you felt like you should tell them, but, No, that is forbidden. You also understand that no matter what your chess rating is, we all make the same errors.

WAR AND CHESS

Most of the people locked up for legal problems, and in most countries in the twentieth century, have had chess sets available to them. However, down through history of the ages, this was not always the case.

In years past prisoners often had to use their ingenuity to come up with chess sets. The pieces might have been made from paper, beads, straw, clay or wood. The board may have been anything from a blanket to a checkered table cloth, a handkerchief, or even a tiled floor.

At one time in the Pawing prison in Warsaw, chess was played when Germany occupied Poland. The pieces were made of bread and the chessboard was marked out with ashes from a fire. If the guards came around un expectantly, the chessmen could be eaten and the ash chessboard simply blown away.

Also, during the second world war, and in a Royal Air Force Prisoners of War camp chess had not been one of the organized activities. That is until a Czechoslovakian by the name of Novotney was placed in the barracks of Stalag Luft 1. He began to give lectures on the game, and tests to see if the others were paying attention to his teachings.

This started an evolution of chess players with each donating what they could to the game. The camp craftsmen were producing chess pieces of some quality and committee's were formed to arrange tournaments between the different barracks. Individual matches were taking place and the participants thought they were doing well. They thought that way until a Canadian joined the group. Brunet was a man of high chess quality and he soon had the others realizing they were just on the outskirts of chess knowledge.

He soon had them playing ladder tournaments and at one time played a simultaneous game with sixteen boards in contention. Apparently even the German guards got to watching the games in progress, during one prolonged game where it could go either way, the guards were so mentally involved, that a British officer escaped.

ALCOHOLIC CHESS

I don't know when this kind of chess game came into being, but it was played on a large board, which instead of using normal chess pieces, it had glasses or bottles of strong liquor. The rule was that when you captured one of your enemies pieces you had to drink it entirely before resuming play. If you became inebriated to the extent you couldn't continue to play the game, you lost. One game that took place in 1898 in Hungary had bottles of Champagne as Kings. The Queen was represented by a bottle of Liebfraumilch. Other pieces were Tokay and the pawns were Vin Rouge. When the players were both so inebriated that neither could play any longer, they left the game as it was, observers found that it apparently had quite an interesting middle game left in the alcohol's wake. It is rumored that Lasker won a game of alcoholic chess by sacrificing his Queen early in the game. The queen was a litre of Cognac.